ONE
FRIGHTFUL
DAY

A MYSTERY

Cover design, interior book design, and eBook design
by Blue Harvest Creative
www.blueharvestcreative.com

ONE FRIGHTFUL DAY

Published by Barking Frog
an imprint of BHC Press

Library of Congress Control Number:
2016962150

ISBN-13: 978-1-946006-34-9
ISBN-10: 1-946006-34-3

Visit the authors at:
www.bhcpress.com

OTHER BOOKS IN

BY JUDITH BLEVINS & CARROLL MULTZ

Operation Cat Tale

These Titles Coming Soon

Blue

The Ghost of Bradbury Mansion

White Out

A Flash of Red

Back In Time

TABLE OF CONTENTS

AUTHORS' NOTE

The authors of *One Frightful Day* seek neither to confirm nor refute the existence of Santa Claus. That is left to the personal opinion of their readers. Although there have been unconfirmed sightings of the jolly old elf, the circumstantial evidence set forth in the final chapter of *One Frightful Day* would seem to support the proposition that Santa Claus exists today the same as he has over the last one-thousand years. The authors would welcome personal stories from their readers that would tend to either confirm or refute Santa's existence.

Hopefully, our readers' journey with the R*U*1*2s in *One Frightful Day* will be an enjoyable one—one that will propel them to greater heights. If so, the reader will no doubt find the first novel in the Childhood Legends Series®, *Operation Cat Tale*, to be equally as enjoyable. Books have been, are and will always be our friends.

To Margie Vollmer Rabdau, Dr. Donald A. Carpenter and those who provided the impetus to write this novel, our profound gratitude. Last but not least, to our publisher, BHC Press, we are eternally grateful.

FOREWORD

Our newly formed club, the *Are You One Toos (R*U*1*2s* for short), had close to two dozen members (twenty-two to be exact) ranging in age from five to twelve years old. All the members lived in and around our neighborhood and were instrumental in converting an abandoned apple shed into a terrific clubhouse.

Homer Pearson, Rhymin' Sally's father, gave us permission to use the shed as a clubhouse after Sally, a precocious five-year old, was threatened by a band of thugs. It was approximately a year ago that Sally was rescued from the lawless group, who as it turned out, had been cruising our neighborhood looking for something to steal or destroy. They descended on the apple stand on the edge of the apple orchard manned by Sally and her mother like a swarm of bees. Apparently, the thugs had staked out the stand as a target, and when Sally was left alone while her mother sought to replenish the apple supply, they struck.

The thugs would have made off with the cash drawer had it not been for a group of neighborhood youngsters returning from a school function and who just happened to be passing by the stand. Seeing what was happening, they immediately sprung to Sally's aid. I am proud to say I was part of that group. We struggled with the intruders before the thugs were frightened away by Sally's mother who, after seeing what was taking place, used her cell phone to summon Sally's father. When Sally's father arrived and was told about the heroic actions, he praised us and a bond was forged between the Pearsons and our neighborhood group.

"What can we do to repay you?" Homer Pearson had asked.

"Aww, it was nothing. We don't need to be repaid," I had replied.

However, when Sally's father was persistent and insisted he be given the opportunity to repay us, I pointed to an abandoned apple storage shed that had stood vacant for a number of years in the middle of the Pearsons' apple orchard and said, "We are in the process of forming a club to occupy us for the summer and could use your apple shed as a clubhouse."

"It's yours," Sally's father replied without hesitation. "I'll meet you at the apple shed tomorrow at noon. We, that is the Pearson three, will have lunch waiting for you and your friends and we'll explore what needs to be done to fashion that dilapidated old shed into a suitable clubhouse."

"Yippee!" we all shouted.

The next day, with some of our fellow classmates, neighbors and friends, we descended upon the orchard. There were at least twenty-four in number. And as promised, the Pearsons had lunch waiting. After everyone had settled in, Sally asked each of us, one-by-one, if we were one of the heroes who had rescued her the day before.

"Are you one too?" I remember her asking. And so, it came to pass that the name of our newly formed club was conceived. From that point forward, we would be known as the *Are You One Toos (R*U*1*2s)*. All those present, including Sally, became the coveted charter members.

With the help of Homer Pearson, we furnished the clubhouse with empty packing crates and other odds and ends we gathered from our families. Our mothers took turns providing sandwiches, drinks and snacks. It was cool inside the converted apple storage shed because the apple trees outside provided shade and a persistent breeze wafted through the open door and windows as if on cue.

The clubhouse was soon jammed with an assortment of games and books. During those summer months, Shacoo and I took turns reading to our fellow *R*U*1*2s*. Our seventh grade teacher to be had challenged us to do something over the summer to promote education in our respective neighborhoods. At first, we did this to satisfy the homework assignment but it was not long before we discovered it was not only educational but fun as well.

Everyone looked forward to our reading sessions. The reading sessions not only became a hobby, but an obsession, and needless to say, our parents were delighted that we were not whittling away our time or getting into mischief.

TO OUR INSPIRATION

Cole, Emily, Joey, Kate, Kirsten, Logan, Taran, Trenton, Bridget, Hannah, Irina and Caroline.

THE
CHILDHOOD LEGENDS™
SERIES

ONE
FRIGHTFUL
DAY
A MYSTERY

BY **JUDITH BLEVINS** &
CARROLL MULTZ

BARKING
FROG

LIVONIA, MICHIGAN

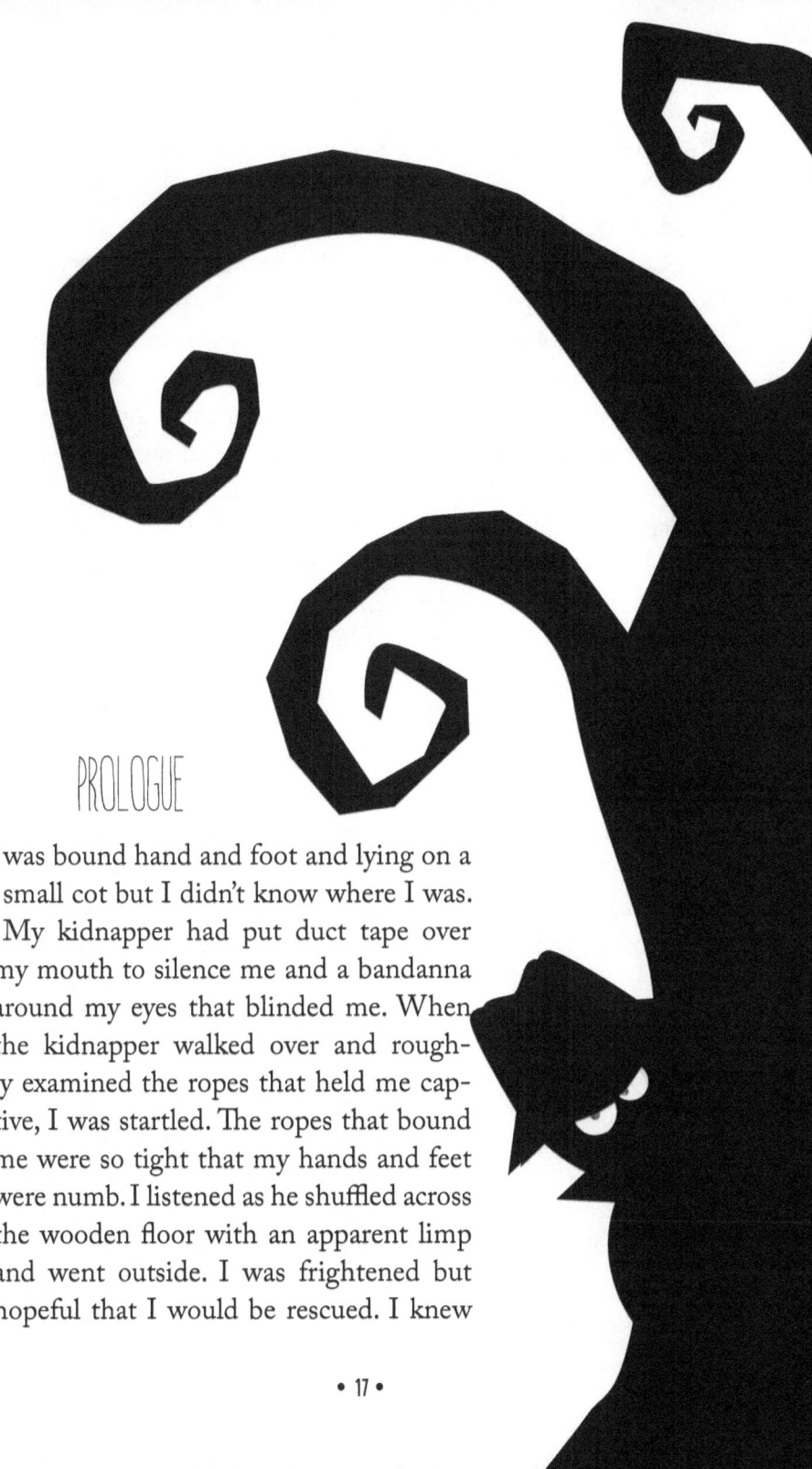

PROLOGUE

was bound hand and foot and lying on a small cot but I didn't know where I was. My kidnapper had put duct tape over my mouth to silence me and a bandanna around my eyes that blinded me. When the kidnapper walked over and roughly examined the ropes that held me captive, I was startled. The ropes that bound me were so tight that my hands and feet were numb. I listened as he shuffled across the wooden floor with an apparent limp and went outside. I was frightened but hopeful that I would be rescued. I knew

Tank had last seen me hiding behind the Nissan Outback in Atkinson's driveway about half-way up the block. I hoped he had sounded the alarm.

As I struggled with the ropes that bound my hands trying to loosen them, I kept thinking of my parents knowing they would be frantic with worry. It was my concern for them that gave me the resolve to keep trying to free myself from my bondage even though at the time it appeared futile. I remained still so as not to alert my abductor. I felt my best chance of survival was to remain calm and not give him cause to administer his brand of retribution which I anticipated would be harsh and unyielding. When I refer to my abductor by the male gender, it is because of his appearance, his voice and his mannerisms.

By the way, my name is Shacoo Bandaris. I am a twelve year old seventh grader and attend Woodrow Wilson School in Jefferson City, Iowa. It's obvious I have an unusual first name. After my first day in school and being teased about my name, I asked my mother how it came to be. She said when she was still in high school, she had gone on a senior trip with her classmates to an isolated island in the Pacific. The word "shacoo" in the island's dialect meant "I love you." She said she was so captivated by the natives and culture that she decided if she ever had a daughter she would name her "Shacoo." I often wonder what name either a brother or sister would have been given had I not been an only child.

My mother's name is Katrina but my father and her friends call her Katie; my father's name is Carlo. My father is a biologist and is employed as a lab technician for Chemical Technology Resources, Inc. His company performs forensic analysis on evidence submitted by local law enforcement agencies.

Even now, thinking about what happened back *on that one frightful day* brings tears to my eyes. I can still picture myself hopelessly laying there bound and gagged imagining the worse. If you'd told me I would live to tell about the ordeal, I would have bet a million dollars that there was not even the slightest chance. If I become emotional in the pages that follow, you'll know why. It all started while we were playing hide-'n-seek…

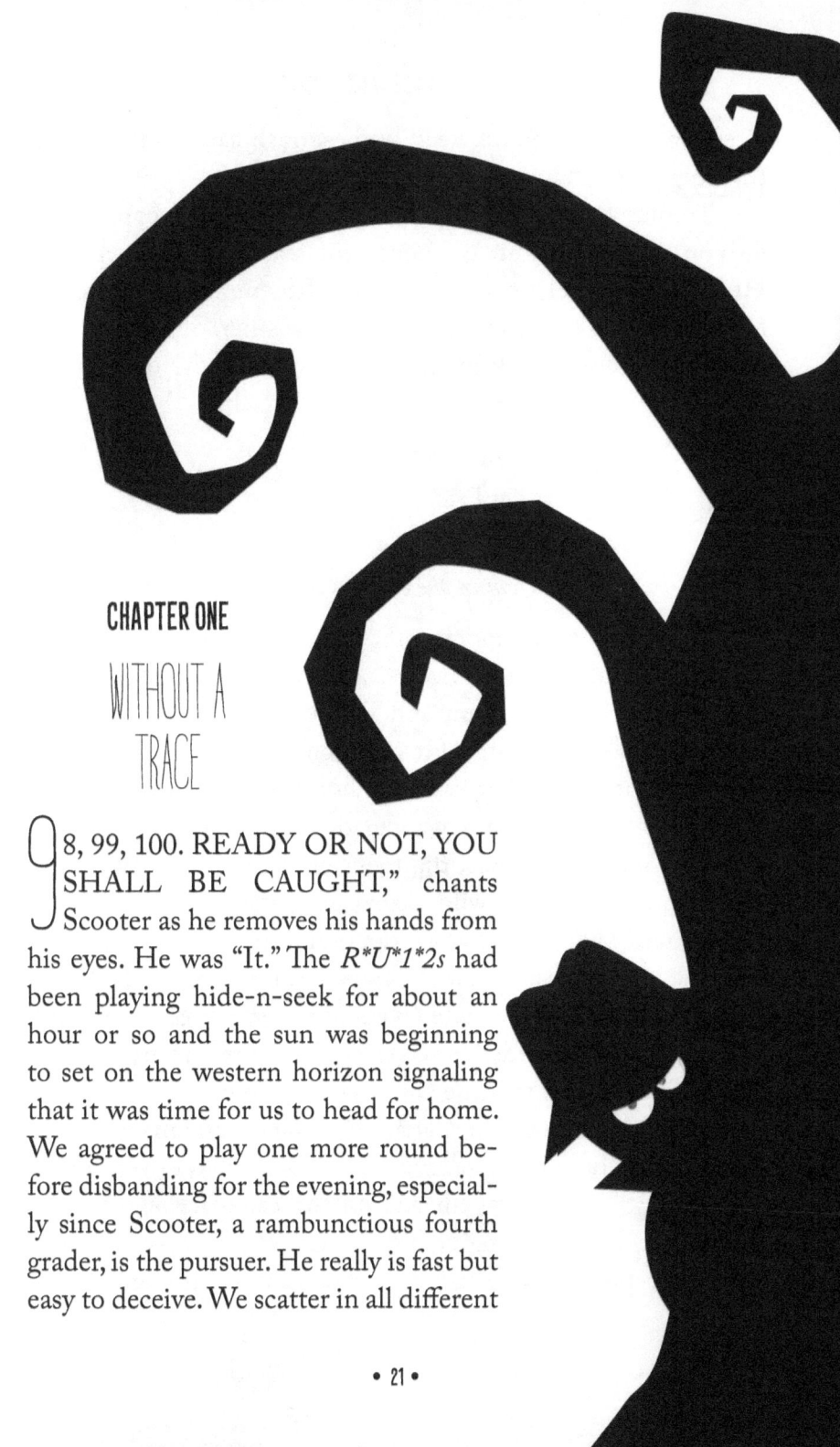

CHAPTER ONE

WITHOUT A TRACE

"98, 99, 100. READY OR NOT, YOU SHALL BE CAUGHT," chants Scooter as he removes his hands from his eyes. He was "It." The *R*U*1*2s* had been playing hide-n-seek for about an hour or so and the sun was beginning to set on the western horizon signaling that it was time for us to head for home. We agreed to play one more round before disbanding for the evening, especially since Scooter, a rambunctious fourth grader, is the pursuer. He really is fast but easy to deceive. We scatter in all different directions hiding behind trees, bushes, trash cans and anything that might shield us from Scooter's detection.

Scooter begins the search in somewhat of a hap-hazard fashion as is his custom and hence, the reason for his ineptness. He literally stumbles over five year old Rhymin' Sally hiding behind a lilac bush and reaches out and tags her. She slowly and dejectedly ambled back to home base to await the outcome of the game. As she waits, she mumbles to herself,

Someday I'll be big and fast.
They'll be sorry as I run past.
I'll make it home free with time to spare
And then look 'em in the eye and say 'so there!'

Scooter, now with more confidence, darts from place to place looking behind trees and bushes, scouring the neighbors' property, and finally spots Sonny and Toby crouched behind a swing on the Bailey's front porch. He ceremoniously tags each of them and sends them back disgustedly to home base. In the meantime, noticing that Scooter has wandered too far away from home base, Mohawk, Pineapple, the twins (Dusty and Rusty), Carly and then Genius make wild dashes for home base and make it "home free." That leaves two holdouts and the ones Scooter considers the most evasive, namely, Tank and me.

Scouring the immediate area and not spotting either Tank or me, Scooter expands his search and ventures far from home base. When he sees that the coast is clear, Tank dashes out from his hiding place beside the Carrington's garage and makes a bee-line home without being tagged. "Tain't over 'till it's over," I hear Scooter say, "I still have Shacoo on the run. She ought to be easy to tag." I creep from one hiding place to another in order to avoid detection. I try to stay one step ahead of him and out of his reach. I am now far removed from home base which proves to be my downfall.

After long minutes of frantic searching and even announcing I could come in safe, as I was later told, I just seemed to have vanished. Frustration apparently turns to panic and the rest of the *R*U*1*2s* join Scooter in an attempt to locate me. It was out of character for me, according to them, to play mind-games that would cause others to worry and worry they did. Genius and Tank, my two best friends, and incidentally, also seventh graders and classmates of mine, were apparently particularly concerned. What happened next, I later pieced together mostly from the statements of my fellow *R*U*1*2s*.

TANK AND GENIUS HASTILY made their way to the spot where I had last been seen. They apparently scoured the area searching for even a hint of my whereabouts. When they arrived at the Atkinson's driveway, they circled the parked vehicle, looking in all directions and even underneath the car.

When Genius bent to inspect the area at the rear of the car, he noticed something twinkling as the rays of the setting sun struck the object. He reached under the back bumper of the car and retrieved a charm bracelet belonging to me. He knew it was mine because he had given it to me as a Christmas present the previous year. The bracelet's charms consisted of a cat to commemorate the *R*U*1*2s* previous year's encounter with a cat burglar; a small silver star because my favorite night sky was shooting stars; a bicycle because Genius often gave me rides on the back of his bike; and a small puffed heart signifying Genius' professed affection for me. He said he knew I would not have been careless enough to lose the bracelet as it was very near and dear to me. He also said he could only surmise that I had not left it there willingly. The clasp looked to him to be damaged perhaps in some kind of struggle. According to Tank, Genius hastened over to him and showed him the bracelet. Tank said he was also aware of my fondness for the bracelet. The two apparently became quite concerned and began to think the worse.

Concern, they later said, soon evolved into desperation, as the sun began to set. The situation didn't look promising, he said, and they knew time was not in their favor. Tank reputedly had asked Genius, "Are you thinking what I'm thinking?" He said he did not receive an immediate response and nervously shifted from one foot to the other while jamming his hands deep in the pockets of his rugged coveralls waiting for Genius' response. Genius just shrugged his shoulders and finally with a raspy, husky voice said, "Your guess is as good as mine. I sense something terrible has happened to Shacoo. I feel it in my bones. We need to get help and pronto!"

"I'll go get Dad." Tank had said, "He'll know what to do. You stay here and keep a look out for Shacoo. I'll be back as soon as I can." Tank then apparently sprinted frantically in the direction of his home.

Tank's father, Liam O'Malley, is a sergeant on the city police force. He had successfully engineered Tank's rescue from *The Cat*, a burglar who had ravaged our neighborhood for almost a year and had been captured just six months before. *The Cat* had taken Tank hostage during a daring escape attempt but was out-witted by law enforcement and finally subdued. As Tank headed towards his house, he said he could not help but relive the entire "cat episode." He knew *The Cat* was still in prison but still something very familiar kept haunting his thoughts. He said he wondered if *The Cat* might have had something to do with my disappearance.

In the meantime, the other members of the *R*U*1*2s* had gathered in Atkinson's driveway clamoring to know what had happened to me. Genius, in a hushed but concerned voice, I was told, had said, "We cannot find Shacoo and we're worried something bad has happened to her. Tank went to get his dad. We think Shacoo was hiding behind this car since we found her damaged charm bracelet under the back fender." As they began to peer beneath the car, Genius, I was told, said, "Please don't come much closer. We don't want to disturb anything until we determine Shacoo's whereabouts. Preserving the scene is something Tank's father would want us to do. There may be important clues that will help in locating Shacoo if indeed something terrible has happened to her." When Cupcake began to tremble, Genius purportedly said reassuringly, "It is important that we all remain calm. To become upset will not solve anything." Inside, Genius said he felt an uneasiness that would soon become all-consuming.

The other *R*U*1*2s*, beginning to experience the same sensation, apparently began whispering among themselves seeking an explanation. As darkness set in, Genius told everyone to return to their homes so as not to worry their parents. Mrs. Atkinson said later that she noticed the commotion in the yard and sensed something was amiss. She then said she stepped out onto the porch and asked if there was a problem. Genius apparently hastened over to her and replied, "Mrs. Atkinson, Shacoo is missing. We were playing hide-n-seek and she was last seen in your driveway hiding behind your car. Tank went to get his dad and I'm staying here just in case. Since we didn't see her around your house, we assume she is not inside. Besides, it would not be like Shacoo to just mysteriously disappear. I don't suppose by any chance that you've seen her, have you?"

"Why, no, I haven't. I've been busy fixing dinner and would have seen her had she come inside. Nonetheless, I'll look around just in case. Have you checked the garage?" Genius apparently nodded his head indicating that he had.

As she started inside, Genius asked, "Mrs. Atkinson, will you please call my parents and also Mr. and Mrs. Bandaris and explain to them what has happened? The Bandarises should probably come over and see for themselves. Maybe by some quirk, Shacoo has returned home and we are making something out of nothing."

"Oh, my, yes. Let's pray that is the case." Mrs. Atkinson then said she agreed to make the calls. Mr. Atkinson, having overheard the conversation between the two, immediately went out to help Genius search for me and for any clues that would aid in my discovery.

SERGEANT O'MALLEY SAID HE knew his son would not sound an alarm if there wasn't ample reason for concern. So, before leaving for the Atkinson's residence, he placed a call to my parents to make sure I wasn't with them. Learning that I wasn't, Sergeant O'Malley said he called in the report of a missing child. Sergeant O'Malley and Tank, I learned later, drove the two blocks to the Atkinson's residence. Sergeant O'Malley declared the Atkinson's driveway a possible crime scene and had Genius and Tank remove themselves to the Atkinson's front porch and remain there until after the crime scene had been carefully combed for possible evidence.

Within a short period, two cruisers apparently pulled up next to the driveway and four uniformed officers exited their vehicles and approached Sergeant O'Malley. Mr. Atkinson had turned on the flood lights to illuminate the driveway so that there would be plenty of light to search for clues, if any there be. After carefully searching for over an hour, the police team apparently came up empty-handed except for the broken charm bracelet and a right-hand leather glove found in the bushes next to the Atkinson residence.

Sergeant O'Malley called in a request for a fingerprint team to appear on the scene to dust the rear of the vehicle on the off-chance there might be fingerprints to identify who may have touched the vehicle and presumably determine who, if anyone, was involved in my disappearance. He, it was later said, requested that our entire family be fingerprinted in order to eliminate their prints and also to obtain a sample of my prints from something I had handled in my home. To that end, a member of the police team, who had responded to the scene, immediately escorted my mother home to retrieve an item which would provide a sample of my prints.

My mother, I later learned, broke down and cried as she showed the officer my room. She, I was later told, could not be consoled. So, Officer Feldman Lancaster let her be by herself and scoured my room on his own for an item or items that he thought might be the best objects from which to retrieve my fingerprints and maybe even my DNA. He, I was told, selected a hairbrush and a note book that were lying on my bed. He carefully bagged the items in separate evidence bags and sealed them.

Officer Lancaster, it was said, then returned to the kitchen where my mother sat worried and said in a soft voice, "Mrs. Bandaris, we know this must be difficult for you but please trust we will do everything within our power to locate Shacoo and return her to you. Although our city is relatively small, we have one of the best police departments in the state. Many of our specialized technicians have been recognized for their police work, and in fact, other police agencies from around the state have been trying to lure our personnel away. I can tell you truthfully that, to the person, there are none more competent. What I'm saying is, if it's any comfort to you, rest assured you will have the best of the best at your disposal."

My mother, wringing a tissue nervously in her hands and nodding her head, I was later told, quietly replied, "I will count on it."

Officer Lancaster, my mother later said, gently took her by the arm and guided her towards the front door so that she could let him out and lock the door behind her. He asked, as she stood in the doorway, "Do you desire to return to the Atkinson's residence or would you prefer to remain here?"

"At this point, I don't know what I should do," she reputedly said. My mother was obviously distraught and consumed with uncertainty. Knowing her, she would do whatever she needed to do in order to obtain my safe return. She, I was later told, was seeking guidance and felt Officer Lancaster was someone upon whom she could rely.

"It's been my experience that there is usually a phone call or two from the kidnapper outlining his demands if indeed your daughter has been abducted. For now, I would suggest that you come back with me to the Atkinson's residence and we'll confer with Sergeant O'Malley. My guess is he's on top of the situation and is formulating a plan of action as we speak. Are you up to it?"

"Yes. Whatever it takes to get Shacoo back, I'll do. Thank you again for your kindness and understanding." With her head down and trying to control the sobs, I was told, she grabbed her coat and headed for the door.

"I have children of my own so I can relate to what you're going through. Let's get on back." Hesitating momentarily, Officer Lancaster then said, "It is possible Shacoo may not be in harm's way at all and there very well may be an innocent explanation as to her whereabouts. Normally, we would wait a much greater period of time to give a reported missing person time to return. However, at Sergeant O'Malley's insistence and that of the R*U*1*2s, we are not risking your daughter's safety and are treating her disappearance as a possible kidnap. It is always best to error on the side of caution."

When they arrived back at the Atkinson's residence, Sergeant O'Malley greeted them. He apparently said to my mother and father, "I'm going to request that the two of you return home. I'm sending Officer Lancaster back with you. It is possible you may receive a telephone call from the abductor if in fact Shacoo has been abducted. Officer Lancaster will instruct you on how to answer the telephone should that happen. He has a recording device that he will attach to an extension so that any in-coming calls can be monitored and recorded. He will also give you instructions on how to respond. He will stay with you throughout the night and then be relieved by another of our officers in the morning. Our experience is that you will not receive a call tonight. It's a game criminals play to taunt their victims and make them more desperate and pliable. Maintain your composure and do not panic—especially if you should hear Shacoo's voice on the other end of the line. If she knows her parents are confident and certain, she will be also." Then turning to Officer Lancaster, he said, "Feldman, you know what to do."

Officer Lancaster responded, "Indeed I do. Mr. and Mrs. Bandaris, come with me. Let me drive you both home."

My parents, I was told, took another quick look around as if somehow expecting to see me magically appear. They knew it was probably futile but they had to make the effort anyway. Disbelief was still written across their faces. They then climbed into the blue and white police cruiser and left with Officer Lancaster to begin what must have been a long agonizing wait. In the interim, my father later told me, they would be calling on a power greater than them to assist in the impending ordeal.

TANK AND GENIUS WERE still huddled together on a swing on the Atkinson's porch when my parents left. Both boys were visibly shaken and paralyzed with fear for my safety, I was later told. They then talked among themselves. Who would abduct Shacoo? If money was what the kidnapper was after, he picked the wrong victim. Shacoo's parents weren't wealthy, so money did not appear to be the object. The boys were apparently at a loss as to motive. As expected, so were the authorities. Wouldn't Genius, whose parents were physicians and pretty well to do, be a more likely target, they speculated. Or how about Tank, whose father was a well-known police officer. Wouldn't he also be a better target? If it wasn't money, then what was it?

When the boys saw that the on-site investigation had been completed and the law enforcement officers had cordoned off the area with yellow tape warning by-passers not to cross into the taped area, they said they decided it was time to leave. They said they then slowly started up the street towards their respective homes distressed and downtrodden. They said they hoped for the best but feared for the worse. Genius said he was particularly reluctant to leave because this was the last known place where I had been. Tank apparently had to nudge Genius along. Genius said he felt that by staying he would be closer to me than if he left. He said Tank had uttered words of encouragement as they meandered down the street. Genius recounted that he would turn and look back occasionally towards the Atkinson's driveway unable to come to grips with the reality of my disappearance. Later he would say, none of it made any sense. Regardless of the way it appeared, he said, he still had to think positive and do everything he could to insure my safe return. That was Genius!

ONCE HOME, MY PARENTS were instructed on what to say if and when the ransom call came. Officer Lancaster apparently attached a small recording device to the telephone and the long anticipated wait ensued. My mother said she busied herself fixing a light dinner for the three of them. I was later told that Officer Lancaster took my father aside while they waited and asked him if he knew of any reason why someone would want to kidnap me.

As I indicated previously, my father was employed by a local laboratory as a research technician. He had a degree in biotechnology and worked mainly in the field of DNA research. The company he worked for, as I also related, conducted testing for local law enforcement agencies on DNA samples collected from various and sundry crime scenes. He made a respectable living but was not wealthy by any stretch of the imagination. Even though the reason for my kidnapping remained a mystery, my father said he was beginning to suspect that it might have something to do with his job.

At dinner, my mother later said, the three of them sat around the kitchen table conversing over possible reasons for my kidnapping. She said they were unable to come up with a logical explanation. My father, on the other hand, said he was beginning to connect the dots. That very day, he recalled, the laboratory had received samples of DNA from the Jefferson City Police Department taken from the scene of the recent bank robbery wherein the robber had made off with an estimated $500,000 in cash. Apparently, the robber had a sneezing fit right in the middle of demanding the tellers to give him all of their cash. At least, that was what the teller told the police.

Samples of the mucus ejected from the sneezing episode, it was later determined, were left on the counter of the teller cage even though the robber wore a mask. The samples were subsequently collected by the JCPD's crime scene team and sent to Chemical Technology Resources, Inc., my father's employer, for analysis.

My father was the senior analyst at CTR and had the reputation of being the most competent of all the lab technicians. As a result, I later learned, he was assigned to conduct the DNA analysis of the mucus samples recovered at the bank. The testing was to be conducted by him the following morning. Could obtaining the identity of the bank robber be a key piece of evidence in solving the mystery as to my disappearance? He said the question resonated in his mind. The more he wondered the more he comprehended, he said. It was beginning to make sense—though in some distorted and satanical way. He concluded, the abductor was likely the robber and trying to use leverage to obtain my father's cooperation in distorting the results and thus in hiding the robber's true identity.

My father said he was reluctant to pass this information on to Officer Lancaster for fear, if his suspicions were confirmed, that the revelation would put me in even greater danger. The prudent thing for now, he said, was to keep his fears to himself and adjust to the changing circumstances as they unfolded.

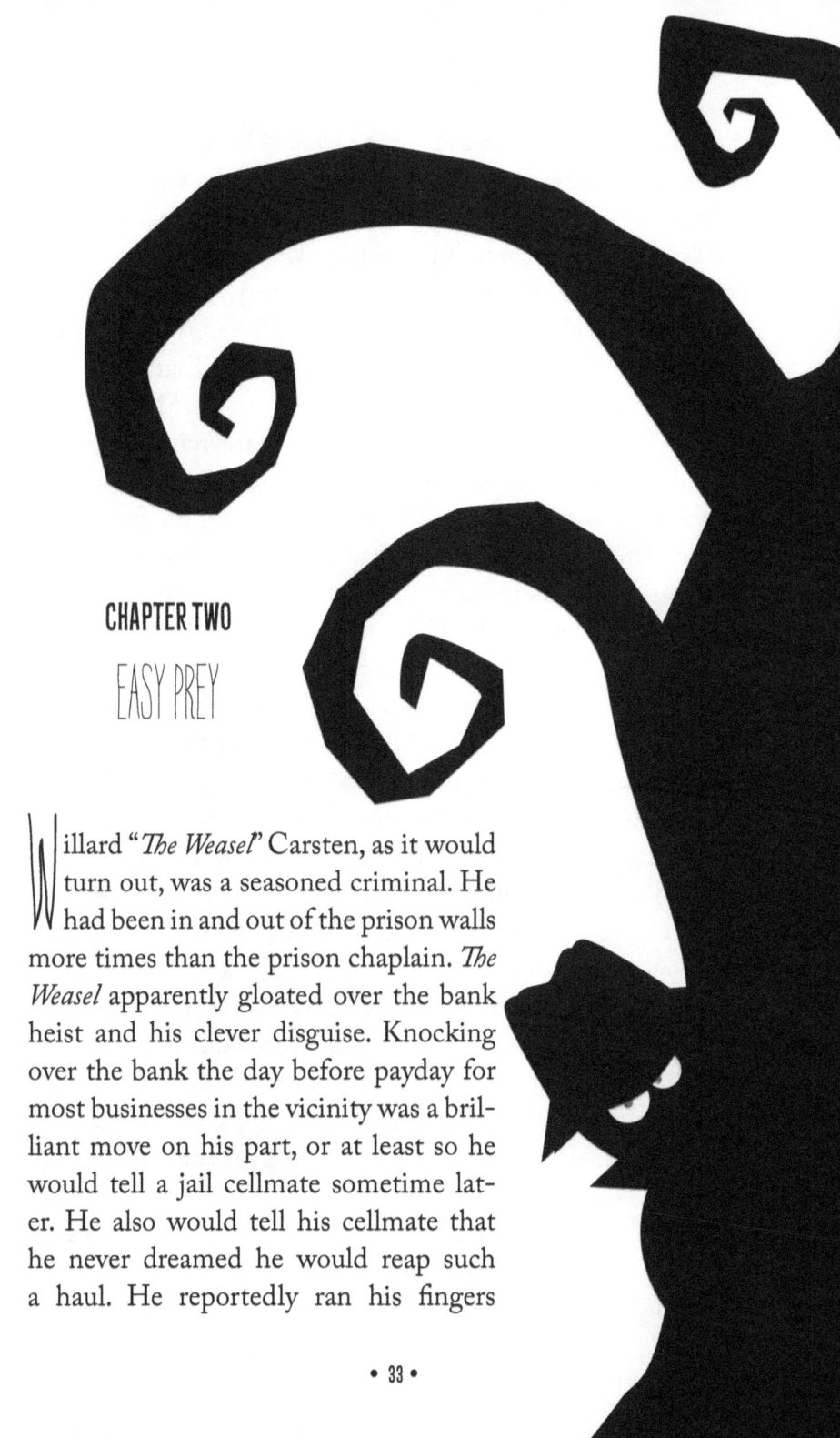

CHAPTER TWO

EASY PREY

illard "*The Weasel*" Carsten, as it would turn out, was a seasoned criminal. He had been in and out of the prison walls more times than the prison chaplain. *The Weasel* apparently gloated over the bank heist and his clever disguise. Knocking over the bank the day before payday for most businesses in the vicinity was a brilliant move on his part, or at least so he would tell a jail cellmate sometime later. He also would tell his cellmate that he never dreamed he would reap such a haul. He reportedly ran his fingers through the cash like it was running water. He also told his cell-mate he now knew how Midas had felt. Later he would say his joy was short lived when he began remembering his sneezing episode at the bank, something he had always done when he became excited even as a child. "Drat it anyway," he said to himself. "This would have been a clean caper if it hadn't been for me leaving my DNA at the scene, drat, drat, drat!" That's when he began to hatch a plan.

The Weasel said he knew only all too well the routine for testing evidence as he had traveled down that road on more than a few occasions as a seasoned criminal. This was not his first rodeo, he would later tell his cellmate. He also related that he knew who was often called as the expert witness by prosecutors to explain the results and method of DNA testing and how the results led to the positive identification of a perpetrator. Yes, he said, he knew only too well because he had been nailed a few years earlier by my father's expert testimony regarding the results of a DNA analysis that had linked him to a crime that had netted him a short but unpleasant prison term at the state penitentiary.

Several of *The Weasel's* buddies had also been fingered and convicted as a result of my father's expertise. For that reason, *The Weasel*, the authorities later learned, had done some research on his own and had found out "everything there was to know" about our family, including me. He bragged he had staked out our residence and knew the routine of each family member. He allegedly kept a notebook in his shirt pocket and scribbled notes as he observed our family's comings and goings. His dogged determination made the paparazzi look like fledglings, at least according to him.

Although *The Weasel* didn't know how he was going to seek revenge for what my father had put him through, he just knew he would. Now that the one and the same, Carlo Bandaris, my father, could provide another nail for the coffin, so to speak, he had more than an axe to grind. His motive was no longer mere vengeance but a way to blackmail my father and dissuade him from making a positive analysis that would put him away forever. *The Weasel* later said he knew my father could not be bought. It was common knowledge, my father's testimony was not for sale. But, according to *The Weasel's* reasoning, persuasion could take a different and more effective form—kidnap me and hold me for ransom not in exchange for money but in exchange for my freedom and ultimately his. What father wouldn't falsify a lab report in exchange for the life of his daughter? *The Weasel* now had an ace up his sleeve, by his account, and a card he would not be reluctant to play.

The Weasel said he was fairly sure he had left incriminating DNA at the crime scene (the bank). He said he knew it would be submitted for analysis and that it would ultimately be traced to him because of his previous criminal involvement and retention by the authorities of samples of his DNA. He said he was also fairly sure that my father would be the lab technician assigned to do the testing and that the results, without question, would point in his direction. More importantly, *The Weasel*, it was later determined, had already conceived of a fool-proof way to kidnap me and had already determined my routine and habits.

Watching the *R*U*1*2s* playing hide-n-seek and following my every move, he determined it would be an easy score. When he drove past the Atkinson's residence and spotted me and my path to the car in the drive in front of the open garage, he correctly surmised that the view from the residence was blocked by the vehicle and he could thereby avoid detection. He also said he observed the high foliage that blocked the view on the other side of the vehicle. That would block the view of nosey neighbors, he said. He said he also saw me squat behind the car which was parked with the rear closest to the open garage door.

Even though it was dusk, *The Weasel* apparently detected the open rear door in back of the empty garage. Going around the block and down the alley, it was later determined, *The Weasel* parked in the alley behind the Atkinson property, and by way of an unlocked gate, made his way to the garage. He would later brag that he slinked through the open rear door and to the front of the garage where he easily seized his "unsuspecting victim." And you know who that was!

With a hand muffling my screams, he carried me to his vehicle where he made his undetected get-away. He stopped in the alley behind a vacant lot in the adjacent block and there bound and gagged me before heading for the outskirts of Jefferson City. In case you're wondering, I did try to resist. I kicked and scratched with all my strength and tried desperately to wiggle away. Although *The Weasel* was scrawny, he was strong and I was no match for his determination.

THE WEASEL, I WAS told later, was banking on the fact that my father would falsify the DNA results to save me but, being a realist, he suspected that after I was released, my father would likely recant explaining the reason for the inaccuracy. If that were to occur, *The Cat* reasoned, he would have gained nothing, only prompt the authorities to add still another serious crime to the charges.

The Weasel's scheme included a stop-gap measure for just such an occurrence; one, as it would turn out, that would remain a secret until needed.

The Weasel had to make sure, after my abduction, that he had not been followed. He followed a zig-zag pattern out of town and took me to an abandoned shack at a well site on the outskirts of town that had been used by a drilling crew until the well ran dry a few years before. He knew about it, he would say later, because he, at one time, had been employed as a roughneck by the drilling company before it ultimately declared bankruptcy. The site was obviously selected because it was isolated and away from the watchful eyes of the public.

The Weasel had picked up some valuable computer skills, the authorities later learned, during his various stints in prison and he knew how to obtain cell phone numbers. My father's cell phone number was in *The Weasel's* notepad. Retrieving it, he stopped at a telephone booth at a nearby convenience store and dialed my father's cell number.

My father said he was surprised when his cell phone began to ring, and said later, he never suspected the kidnapper would be on the other end. Not expecting the kidnapper to be the caller, he answered it. "Hello, this is Carlo."

The Weasel apparently replied, "Do not do or say anything to alert anyone near you that this is *the call* you've all been waiting for. If you understand simply say 'Yes.'"

"Yes."

"Good. There are two rules to remember. Rule number one is that I call the shots and you do as I say. Not the other way around! Savvy? Rule number two is that you never tell me 'no.' In other words, if you do exactly as I instruct you, your daughter will be released unharmed. Are you in agreement with that scenario?"

"Yes."

When my father left my mother and Officer Lancaster to take the call on his cell phone, he said both followed him to the other room. My father said he raised a hand signaling everything was all right and my mother and Officer Lancaster walked back to the kitchen allowing him to speak in private. Even though

Officer Lancaster later said he was suspicious, he apparently said nothing. He said he didn't want to alarm my mother so he continued to converse with her all the while straining, although unsuccessfully, to hear my father's end of the telephone conversation. My father, however, deliberately had moved to the far end of the study and spoke in a hushed tone so as to make it impossible for any part of his conversation to be overheard.

"I have your daughter. She is safe—for now. My demands are simple. I am the one who robbed the local bank earlier today and I suspect you have the samples of DNA I left at the bank. My profile is on file. You are to falsify the results. Otherwise, you give me few options. Do I make myself clear?"

"Yes."

"Do you agree to do so?"

"Yes, but…"

"Ah! Ah! Ah! The only word you are allowed to speak is 'Yes.' As far as releasing your daughter, when I'm sure you have painted yourself into the proverbial corner, she will be released unharmed. If you double-cross me by later coming forward with the truth, I know where you live and I will not hesitate to add you and your wife to my list of victims. Do you understand that?"

"Yes."

My father said his heart skipped a few beats and he had a sick feeling in the pit of his stomach. He said he could feel beads of sweat began to form on his forehead and he felt his face become flush. He was not sure how long he could keep up the charade. He just knew he had no real choice—at least not then.

"I will be scanning the newspapers daily waiting for the 'all clear' sign from you. You may now speak a number. In days, how long will it take to complete the analysis of the sample and submit a report? Just one number please."

"Two."

"When you are finished with the analysis I want you to tell the press, 'We were unable to match the DNA sample to any known criminal in our data base.' When I see those words in print, I will release your daughter. Do you agree with the plan?"

"Yes."

"I will not make the obligatory call demanding money, there is no reason to and that would just muddy up our arrangement. Remember your daughter's life is at stake and is now in *your* hands. Incidentally, I'm not a patient man so don't delay and I need to tell you that I spook easily so don't try anything foolish." With that, *The Weasel* apparently abruptly hung up.

According to my mother, after my father hung up, he returned to the kitchen looking flushed and remote. He would later say he was an honorable man but if my life was at stake and whether right or wrong, he would not hesitate to compromise his principles and do whatever it took to preserve my life or the life of any other family member. Noticing my father's appearance, my mother said she had asked him, "Is everything all right? The call wasn't about Shacoo, was it?"

"No, not at all," my father apparently answered and then, according to my mother, added, "It involves some complications at work. I'll take care of them later." My mother said she had no reason not to believe my father and began clearing the dishes and cleaning up the kitchen. Officer Lancaster and my father then went into the living room to await the "anticipated call" which, of course, had already come. Officer Lancaster said later he suspected all was not right but decided not to say anything for fear it would only aggravate the situation. My parents, he said, were already under enough stress.

At midnight, Officer Lancaster advised my parents that it was okay to go to bed. He said he would stand by and listen for the telephone while they slept. My parents thereupon apparently retired to their bedroom. My father said he felt guilty about the deception. He said he had never kept secrets from my mother and said he wasn't about to do so. So, he said, he took my mother in his arms and related to her the contents of the conversation he had just had with the kidnapper. He apparently also asked for her pledge of secrecy for the time being, and because dishonesty was against his nature, he wanted her unconditional approval before embarking upon the fraudulent scheme he was about to undertake. He then told her, knowing it may look uncaring, that he had to return to work the next day in order to get the DNA analysis completed within the allotted time frame and skew the results. She, he said, nodded her understanding and approval. My mother said she sobbed well into the night wondering how it would all end. Both prayed, she said, they were doing the right thing.

The next morning an Officer Sanford relieved Officer Lancaster at our home. My father said he told the officer he had to leave for work. He said he told him he had to analyze a bank robber's DNA and that the authorities couldn't wait. "Time was of the essence regarding this particular case." If he was able to match the DNA to a known sample, he had said, the police could post an APB (all-points bulletin) and hopefully catch the robber before he or she could escape and/or commit other robberies. My father also stated that, because of the summer vacation scheduling, the staff was short-handed and no one else was available to perform the analysis which, as it turned out, was the truth.

Once at work, my father said he began the comparison process. He said he split the samples into two vials. In one vial, he added contaminants to distort the outcome. However, he preserved the second vial and froze it and labeled it "John Doe." He said he did this as a safety measure in the event he should need it later to prove the identity of the true bank robber and the abductor of his daughter. He said he would not compromise my life in order to put a thief behind bars. The trade-off was not open for debate, he said. If he, that is my father, ended up in jail, that was a small price to pay for my safe return. Once commenced, the entire comparison process would take the better part of the day.

When the contaminated vial was analyzed and no match was made, my father submitted his findings to the police department. The public was aware that DNA had been collected at the scene of the bank robbery so law enforcement, it was revealed, felt compelled to announce that they could not match the DNA, and, therefore, had reached a dead end with respect to the DNA sample. Both the electronic and print media reported the inability of the authorities to make a match, and therefore, the identity of the bank robber remained an unsolved mystery. With the perpetrator still at large, it was said, even the most trusting were locking their doors.

As promised, *The Weasel* had been watching the newspaper for the "all clear signal." He apparently was delighted when he saw it. He would say later he was "getting pretty sick and tired of being sick and tired," especially of the rag-tag shack where he was hiding considering he had approximately $500,000 that was "burning a hole in his pocket." *The Weasel*, after reading the newspaper account reporting the DNA analysis and negative results, called my father. I could hear only bits and pieces of *The Weasel's* end of the conversation with my father. After he ended the call, he untied my hands and ankles and removed the tape from my mouth. However, he did leave the bandana over my eyes and tried to disguise his voice when he talked to me. I had already heard his voice when he talked to my father and knew I could identify his voice later if I was called upon to do so. Apparently, by keeping my eyes covered, he thought I would be unable to identify him later.

THE WEASEL, ALTHOUGH A common thief, took pride in his occupation. He had planned ahead and had stocked the shack with food supplies and other necessities to last at least a two week period in the event something went terribly wrong with his plan. He congratulated himself for having so much insight and foresight. The inadvertent discharge of DNA at the bank was an unfortunate occurrence, granted, and perhaps he should have anticipated it, but the repercussions were stifled by my abduction. At least that was his reasoning as we would later learn. He, indeed, was a true professional. No wonder he was held in high esteem by his peers.

Now that he was in the clear, *The Weasel* figured he could proceed with his getaway. He told me he had no intention of staying at the shack or of releasing me until he was a safe distance away. In order to execute his plan, he said he felt he would have to obtain a better vehicle. Having an unlimited supply of money in his possession that was burning a hole in his pocket, he bragged, he would just out-and-out buy a new one. The next morning, he, in my absence, went to the Volkswagen dealership. He said he had seen advertisements that the Passat was "the car of the year" and the gas mileage "was much better than the average." *The Weasel* not only wanted a luxury vehicle, but in his mind he truly felt he deserved not just any car but "the car of the year." What the heck, he could afford it, he told me before getting into the old beater with the banged up right fender he had purchased at a police auction some years before and headed for town. Before leaving the shack, he tied me to a heavy piece of furniture and put the duct tape back over my mouth. He did not mistreat me otherwise. As I said before, I was careful not to give him any cause to do so. I was given decent meals and enough to drink. For that, I felt grateful.

AFTER I HEARD THE roar of his car engine dissipate and figured he was a safe distance away, I began to devise a way to rid myself of the blindfold that still covered my eyes and prevented me from observing my surroundings. Being blindfolded was the part I didn't like when playing hide-n-seek. Even though I could cheat a little from time-to-time, I was virtually operating in the dark. In truth, that was not really the most perplexing part of my plight. As I said before, I was anxious over what my parents were going through. I knew they would be wild with worry and anticipation. I was more concerned by far for them than I was for myself. I didn't know how I was going to escape. I just knew I had no real choice.

I was tied up so tightly and for so long that my sense of self-preservation was being severely tested. However, despite the odds, I never gave up hope. I was raised Christian and knew that God would answer my prayers. I continuously prayed for deliverance from my plight and the patience to endure the test of time. Having heard the outer door slam and the resulting silence after he drove away, I figured that maybe he had left for good. The thought of being stranded without food or drink, or without the ability to obtain it even if it was in reach, clouded my thinking and I prayed more fervently than ever before that my moment of liberation would be close at hand. I didn't know what was worse; him returning or me being stranded without a life line.

WE WOULD LATER LEARN that *The Weasel* drove straight to Montgomery Auto Sales, a local car dealership, and entered with a swagger. Having boo-coo bucks apparently gave him a high sense of entitlement. He approached a salesman and asked to test drive the Passat. The salesman, later when interviewed, said he looked *The Weasel* up and down and wondered if he was real. "I didn't think he had a dime to buy a cup of coffee let alone one of our expensive automobiles." *The Weasel* couldn't contain his ire any longer, apparently, and seeing the look on the salesman's face, reached into his pockets and pulled out two handfuls of hundred dollar bills. The salesman later said he gasped at the sight of the money.

It so happened, Penny and Kitty Montgomery, charter members of the *R*U*1*2s*, had been spending the morning with their father, Greg Montgomery, owner of the car dealership, while their mother was at the beauty shop. They were just leaving to go home when they said they observed the transaction on the sales floor. They told the police that they stopped in their tracks at the sight of the cash and looked at each other in disbelief especially considering the shabby appearance of *The Weasel*. They didn't think he could have panhandled that much money, they would later say. "Then, how did he get it?" Even at their age, they said, they knew something was not quite right.

"Okay, now do I get to test drive the Volkswagen Passat or do I take my business elsewhere?" *The Weasel* reportedly asked, and stuffing the money back in his pockets, started to walk away.

"Of course, Sir, just let me get the keys and a temporary license plate," the salesman allegedly responded. The salesman would later say, that it mattered not from whence his commission for selling the vehicle came.

"Make it snappy, I ain't got all day," *The Weasel* reputedly barked.

The salesman said he returned in quick order with the keys and installed the temporary license plate on the rear of the silver Passat. He handed the keys to *The Weasel,* and while attempting to point out some of the features on the luxury vehicle, was cut off by *The Weasel* who appeared more than anxious to culminate the transaction. The salesman said he didn't hear what *The Weasel* said under his breath as the two hopped in the vehicle. *The Weasel* drove off the parking lot screeching tires and headed for the downtown area with the salesman sitting in the passenger seat apparently holding on for dear life. *The Weasel* said he told the salesman he liked the car after driving only a few miles, and turning around, headed back to the car lot. The salesman said he was grateful to be back in one piece. He said he was still shaking when *The Weasel* ordered him, "Wrap it up and don't take all day. I'm a busy man you know."

The salesman then reportedly said: "We, of course, will have to fill out the paperwork regarding the transaction, issue the title and prepare other necessary government forms. It won't take long. I'll talk to the manager and see if we can't give you two hundred and fifty dollars as a trade-in for your vehicle. If that's agreeable, we can close the deal."

"Okay, just get going, will ya?" *The Weasel* allegedly responded, "Otherwise, I'll quibble over the chintzy trade-in allowance and we'll both walk away from a near deal disgusted and sad."

PENNY AND KITTY MONTGOMERY had left, and were on their way to the *R*U*1*2s'* clubhouse before *The Weasel* returned to the dealership. When they arrived at the clubhouse, they excitedly told the members who were present what they had just witnessed. They were still in awe at the sight of all the green backs. As it happened, Tank and Genius were also present. When they heard the tale of the cash, they said their curiosity was piqued. They said they concluded it was "the bank money."

"When you left, was the man still there?" Tank reportedly asked Penny and Kitty. Something inside him, he said, told him that the man with the money held the key to solving the mystery of my disappearance.

"I think so," Penny had replied. "He's now taking the car for a test drive."

"What kind of car is it?" Tank then asked.

"It's a silver Volkswagen Passat," Kitty responded.

"Come on, Genius. I think we're onto something," Tank reputedly had said. Genius said he didn't need to be persuaded. He said he was already of the same mind and in no time was mounting his bicycle ready to roll. He said Tank jerked his bike up from the ground and was astride beside him in a single movement. Both boys, I learned, raced toward the car dealership.

When they arrived, Genius said he guarded the bicycles while Tank went in to look for the money man. He said he saw who he believed to be the seedy character the Montgomery sisters had described sitting in a glass enclosed cubicle signing various forms. Tank immediately left to join Genius and the two of them began hatching a plan. Tank, it was decided, would ride ahead in the direction they assumed the suspect would take and stop a few miles up the road. Genius would wait and follow the suspect. If the suspect got too far ahead of Genius, Tank would be in a position to pick up the tail. They correctly assumed the suspect would be heading out of town toward the oil fields judging from his apparel and what appeared to be oil stains on his coveralls.

They didn't have long to wait. The suspect was obviously in a hurry. He rudely demanded that the transaction be concluded. The salesman, hastening his pace to avoid further abuse, had *The*

Weasel sign the forms needed to complete the transaction and then provided him with a temporary title. The salesman recalled saying in his politest tone, "Here you are, I think that should do it. You still have the keys and I had the gas tank filled while we completed the sale. I think you're...."

"Never mind the pleasantries," *The Weasel* reportedly snarled. "Apparently you forget that I'm in a hurry." And with that *The Weasel* briskly grabbed the papers, rushed out of the building and drove away leaving the salesman, the latter would later state, standing in the doorway wiping sweat from his brow. "Good riddance," the salesman said he muttered as he watched *The Weasel* immerse himself in the heavy traffic and disappear in the distance.

Genius was just barely in position, he said, when *The Weasel* drove past. Genius followed him to the parameter of the oil fields. Because of the heavy traffic, he said he was unable to keep pace with *The* Weasel but knew Tank was just up ahead and would take up the chase. Tank, in the meantime, had hidden behind a well pump and was ready to roll when he saw the silver vehicle coming in his direction. The boys, they would later say, were familiar with the terrain as they had ridden their bikes and traveled the vacant roads in the area many times. Tank knew that there was a deserted shack in the direction *The Weasel* was headed. He said he lagged behind in order not to alert *The Weasel* to the fact that he was being followed. As Tank languished waiting for *The Weasel* to get far enough ahead of him, Genius caught up to Tank. Tank said he told Genius, "I'm pretty sure he is headed for the deserted shack we discovered a few months ago when we rode up this road. That would be the ideal hideout. We don't want to get too close and spook him."

"That would be my guess as well. Do you think this may be the culprit who kidnapped Shacoo?" Genius, it is told, replied.

"In all likelihood. Just looking at him gives me the willies. It's obvious that he is the bank robber the authorities are looking for. Nobody walks around in rags with pockets full of money. Whether he is connected to Shacoo's disappearance or not we'll soon find out. Let's wait until dusk when we will not be so easily detected. We can ride a little further but I suggest we park the bikes and walk up to the shack. We can't chance being detected. If he is the kidnapper, no telling what he might do to Shacoo especially if he knows *he* is being shadowed."

"That's my concern, also. Or, what he might do to us if he catches us. Regardless, we don't want to give him cause to panic and do the unthinkable." At the time, Genius said, he was worried about what would happen to me and otherwise "would throw caution to the wind."

The boys said they then sat down to wait for the sun to drop behind the horizon. The oil field was in an obscure location and mostly in desert terrain. There were some meager Joshua trees scattered here and there along with tumble weeds and sage brush. Because of the harsh climate, vegetation was sparse and there were no big trees to hide behind. The boys said they knew they would pretty much be out in the open when they advanced on the shack and an easy target. However, under the veil of twilight, they were confident they could approach without being detected.

After what seemed like an eternity, according to both Tank and Genius, the two finally had the shack in sight. The shack, they knew, was windowless. They knew this from their previous foray into the oil field and inspection of the shack. Not having windows, obviously, simplified their approach. They said they inched their way towards the shack and positioned themselves close to the door in order to hear what was going on inside.

The Weasel had, in the meantime, untied me and removed the duct tape from my mouth. The bandana, however, was still covering my eyes. I had been unable to remove it on my own during my abductor's absence. I began to feel fortunate that I had not been able to do so considering his short absence and unpredictable nature. When Tank and Genius said they heard my voice asking for a drink, they said they were relieved. They said, however, they weren't sure what to do next. Long moments apparently passed and Tank whispered to Genius, "Why don't I go get Dad. We can't do this on our own. We need adult help and the sooner the better. Here's the skinny. I'll summon help. You stay here, in hiding, in case he decides to leave. You stay here and keep out of sight. Keep your eyes and ears open. Just hope he doesn't drive off and take Shacoo with him. You won't be able to keep pace. When he was in slow traffic we could hardly keep up with him let alone now when there's little traffic to contend with. By all means, don't do anything that would cause him to harm Shacoo."

Tank later said that Genius was in a frenzy. When tears began to swell up in Genius' eyes, Tank knew the less that was said the better. Tank said he gave Genius an encouraging pat on the back and told him that he had to be brave. Tank then found his way back to where he had hidden his bike and made a hasty departure homeward. He said he knew time was of the essence and that failure was not an option. My life, he felt, literally hung in the balance. He said he knew there would be no room for error.

Now that *The Weasel* had a dependable vehicle, he said he was determined to put some miles between him and the town before his hideout was discovered. He began packing a box with what meager supplies remained. Genius said later he heard the racket inside the shack and correctly surmised what was happening. Surveying his surroundings, he said, he decided his best bet was to disable *The Weasel's* vehicle. Genius related that he approached the Passat with a plan in mind. He said he would let the air out of at least one tire, and if time permitted, two or more tires to prevent the getaway or at the very least stymie the getaway until Tank brought help. Genius said he then frantically hunted for a small twig that he could use to poke into the air valves of the tires to release the air and thus flatten them. Finding the right size, he selected the right rear tire to flatten figuring that was the least noticeable of the four. He said he had no sooner let the air out of the tire when he heard the shack door open. The door made a loud bang as it slammed against the side of the shack. Genius said he then observed *The Weasel* exit the shack with a cardboard box. He said he watched as *The Weasel* used the remote to open the trunk, place the box inside, close the trunk lid and return to the shack.

Genius said he knew he had to stay out of sight until he heard the door of the shack slam shut so he crawled along the side of the car, made his way to the front and then made a dash for a clump of dense brush just as *The Weasel*, with me in tow, emerged from the shack. Genius later said he could see I had duct tape over my mouth and was blindfolded. He said he watched as *The Weasel* shoved me into the back seat and could hear *The Weasel* order me to lay down and stay low. Genius said his heart raced and he felt helpless. He said he knew he couldn't reveal himself and thus give *The Weasel* another hostage and cause to panic. Instead, he said, he watched intently as the vehicle sped off in the opposite direction of town. Much to Genius's delight, he would later say, he also noticed the right rear tire was almost flat and that the car was beginning to wobble as *The Weasel* tore down the wash-board road. For a while, he said, it was difficult to tell whether it was the rough road or a flat tire that was causing the vibration. He surmised *The Weasel* was wondering the same thing.

Upon concluding the rear tire was flat, *The Weasel* pulled over and ordered me to "stay put" as he thrust open the door and stepped out. He was more than angry and muttered loud enough for me to hear, "A flat tire on a new car. How can it be? You just can't trust anybody anymore, especially car salesmen." He got out of the car and opened the trunk. *The Weasel* was making a lot of racket attempting to retrieve the spare or at least I assume that is what he was doing as I was still blind folded. After much clatter, he began to curse when he discovered the vehicle was not equipped with either a jack or a lug wrench. In a fitful rage, he enumerated all the terrible things that were in store for the salesman who sold him the car and the dealership.

I WAS TERRIFIED NOT knowing what was going to happen now that the vehicle had been disabled. The thought crossed my mind that, because of my proximity, I might become the target of *The* Weasel's wrath. I lay very still hoping not to attract attention to myself or in any fashion provoke *The Weasel's* wrath. Perhaps, *The Weasel* would abandon the car with me in it and catch a ride with a passing motorist. I could then attempt a getaway. Otherwise, I would have to wait and pray.

The Weasel, no doubt, was still operating under the impression that he had not been identified. I say that because upon discovering he did not have the means to change the tire, he decided to return to the dealership and have them deal with the problem. He got back into the driver's seat and growled at me that we had to go back to town. He then removed the duct tape and blindfold and told me that if I tried to escape or alert anyone, I would be the first to die. I believed him. He then turned around and headed towards town driving with a flat tire. His ranting and raving was intermittent. He said he would let the salesman, in no uncertain terms, know what he thought. As he rehearsed what he was going to say, I was exposed to some unfamiliar words and descriptions. If my hands hadn't been tied behind me, I would have plugged my ears. He was saying words I was forbidden by my parents to use—words that even today I would never utter.

Needless to say, the trip back to town was bumpy and the vibration was like being in a cement mixer. I was being tossed every which way. The rubber finally peeled off the rim and when the vehicle hit the pavement the metal rim created a tail of fiery sparks and loud clanking noises. I thought, for someone who didn't want to attract attention, my abductor was producing an awful lot of fireworks. I could see the sparks and hear and feel the metal hit the pavement. I knew it was just a matter of time before the vehicle would become totally disabled as even the toughest vehicle would be unable to survive all the abuse. Reaching civilization and being able to see the traffic and the city limits in the distance, needless to say, provided me with new-found hope.

WHEN WE REACHED THE edge of town, Tank, riding with his father in a police cruiser intercepted us. Tank later told me he recognized my abductor's vehicle and apparently told his father, "Dad, that's him!" Tank's father, he said, performed a police maneuver U-turn and fell in behind the silver Passat with the siren wailing. I, of course, was frightened out of my wits and hung on for dear life as *The Weasel* gunned the engine and zig-zagged his way down the narrow highway.

The Weasel was having a difficult time controlling the disabled vehicle and when he crossed the bridge leading into town he pulled over at the edge of a city park located near the outskirts. There, he abandoned the Passat, and grabbing me by the arm, led me into a dense thicket of underbrush. When we got midway, we came face to face with a large cement culvert spanning a small creek, and forcing me into the culvert, he pushed me along. He obviously had hoped his hiding place would not be discovered. Fortunately for me, I later learned, Tank had kept us in sight and saw exactly where I was being led.

When pursuing the Passat, Tank's father had apparently radioed for backup as three additional cruisers soon joined the chase. They converged on the city park and surrounded the areas at both the entrance and exit of the culvert. Tank's father ordered Tank to retreat to a safe distance away. He then went to the trunk of his cruiser and removed a megaphone.

The day was sweltering hot and Tank's father later said he could feel the sweat streaming down his back as he barked into the megaphone, "You in there come out with your hands up. Ready or not, you shall be caught." *The Weasel* and I scrunched down even lower in the confines of the culvert as it narrowed because of a deposit of sludge which occupied a good part of the space. Our vision was impaired by the darkness inside the culvert and the stench made both of us gag. It appeared *The Weasel* had out-smarted himself this time when he decided to take refuge in the dark culvert in the city park. Now he was trapped and I was trapped with him. There were only two ways out, the front of the pipe where we were then crouched and the back of the pipe some twenty feet away. Both exits were covered by police officers with drawn service revolvers and *The Weasel's* disabled vehicle was now in the custody and control of the authorities.

AFTER THE WEASEL HAD left the shack with me, Genius, would later say, he high-tailed it back to town to summon help and alert the authorities. He, of course, was too late. By the time he arrived, he said, *The Weasel* had already been trapped in the culvert. Genius said he found Tank pacing on the outskirts of the police perimeter and it was then that they shared their experiences from the time they had separated. Tank apparently told Genius about his father intercepting *The Weasel* and giving chase and watching the two of us disappear into the mouth of the culvert. Genius, in turn, related to Tank that it was he who had flattened one of the tires on *The* Weasel's Passat. He said he also told Tank about his mad race back to town after he spotted *The Weasel* leave the shack with me in tow. He related that *The Weasel* had headed in the opposite direction of town but apparently had changed his mind and headed back to town. Tank and Genius, I was later told, stood in silent reflection observing what was taking place and praying that I would be released unharmed.

The Weasel had a firm grasp on the rope around my waist. I had since worn myself out trying to wiggle free. I didn't want to be bound and duct taped again so I finally gave up and just sat with my head resting on arms folded around my knees praying for rescue. I had been held hostage at this point for three full days. I was still frightened but could figuratively as well as literally see light at the end of the tunnel. I knew everything possible was being done to rescue me and figured that it was only a matter of time before I would be freed. My parents later said they knew I was a survivor and would endure the anxious waiting; that everything would turn out all right. I knew I would have to do my part by not doing anything to hamper the rescue efforts. I realized that the hero's role was not mine but that of a power beyond human control. Therefore, I remained calm and pushed all the negative thoughts aside. I remembered my parents always telling me to think positive and that's what I did along with uttering several of my favorite prayers including one to my guardian angel.

THE WEASEL WAS NOT quite as circumspect. Like a trapped animal, he clawed and scraped in every direction looking for an avenue of escape. I could hear frustration in his voice. However, he did have me as a hostage to use as a bargaining chip. I can still hear him shouting at the officers, "You out there! I have the girl. I'm a desperate man. With my record, if I'm convicted it would be a life sentence anyway. Do you follow my drift? All I want is to get out of town. The tire on my car needs to be changed. If you will do that and give me space, I promise no harm will come to the girl and she will be released once I'm clear. You have my word."

Tank's father then spoke into the megaphone. "You leave us no choice. What's your plan to release the hostage?"

"That worked out better than I thought," *The Weasel* uttered under his breath but loud enough for me to hear. He then shouted in a raspy voice, "As soon as I'm sure I'm clear, I will let her go. I have her cell phone and I will give it back to her so she can call you with her location once she is released."

"Okay. We are changing your tire as we speak," Tank's father answered. "I'm clearing the area. My men will move back into the park and give you space to come out. I personally guarantee your safe passage."

"Okay, no tricks. You know the consequences!" *The Weasel* yelled back, with authority in his voice.

"No tricks," Tank's father promised.

A spare tire was retrieved from one of the police cruisers, and within minutes, was installed on the Passat. Tank's father then informed *The Weasel* that the Passat was ready to roll.

Immediately, *The Weasel* grabbed the rope attached to my waist and forced me out of the culvert in front of him using me as a shield. His eyes darted around obviously making sure he was not being lured into a trap or ambush. Apparently having satisfied himself the coast was clear, he ran to his car jerking me behind by the rope.

When Genius and Tank saw me, they said they couldn't control their emotions any longer and cried, "Shacoo, Shacoo!" I turned and caught a glimpse of both of them just before *The Weasel* shoved me into the backseat and closed the door. *The Weasel* then climbed into the front seat and revved up the engine. We burned rubber as *The* Weasel floor-boarded it. We then sped off in the opposite direction from which we had come. The police officers stood watching as we departed, and when I looked out of the rear window, I saw the officers huddle around Tank's father. Later, he would say they were skeptical that *The* Weasel would release me without being forced to do so. The quandary was not what would happen to *The Weasel,* but what would happen to me.

The Weasel's silver Passat sped down the highway past the outskirts of town and out into the open country surrounding Jefferson City. There was an old storage warehouse in the vicinity with which *The Weasel,* it was later determined, was familiar. It apparently was common knowledge that some department stores stored seasonal or over-stocked items there. Warehouse sales would occur there usually on the Friday following Thanksgiving and from time to time during the summer months. The stored items included a supply of display cases and mannequins.

The Weasel pulled into the deserted parking lot, and having exited, locked the doors of the Passat with the child–proof lock. I then watched as he climbed through one of the windows of the warehouse that he had broken out. When he was out of sight, I tried to open the doors of the Passat but, of course, didn't have even the slightest success. The car was one of the newer models equipped with a locking device to keep children safe inside.

What I didn't know was that I could have disengaged the child-proof lock from the door panel on the driver's side of the front seat. I did, however, think about climbing into the front seat and exiting through a door window. However, I was afraid I would be caught in the act and knew there would be dire consequences. It wasn't worth the risk, at least not for now. I wagered there would be other and better opportunities. I just hoped I hadn't squandered my first real opportunity to free myself.

The Weasel apparently was familiar with the layout of the warehouse, and in short order, found exactly what he was looking for—a mannequin my approximate size. Rifling through several boxes of inventory, he found jeans and a shirt very similar to what I was wearing. Gathering up the mannequin and the child-sized clothes, he hurried back to the car and stored the items in the trunk alongside the box of supplies he had brought with him from the shack. He retrieved a loaf of bread, jars of peanut butter and jelly, a flimsy plastic knife and some bottles of water from the box. Once back inside the Passat, he handed me the items and instructed me to make each of us a sandwich. Worried about the consequences if I didn't obey and wanting to retain my strength, I did as I was told. I was famished and eagerly ate my PBJ sandwich washing it down with a bottle of stale water.

AFTER THE WEASEL SPED away, and once out of sight, two police cruisers took up pursuit but stayed outside *The Weasel's* view. Tank's father told me later that they had requested helicopter assistance since it was growing dark. He had obtained my cell phone number from Tank and decided to make one last desperate plea for my release. He dialed my cell number. *The Weasel* had the phone in his shirt pocket along with his own and answered mine on the first ring.

"This is Sergeant O'Malley," I could hear him say, "You are no doubt far enough away now to safely release the hostage. You have no reason to keep her. That is part of our deal. My suggestion is that you pull over and let her out of the vehicle, unharmed. You have not been followed as you can clearly see. Your compliance with this request will certainly bode well for you should you, by some quirk, be caught and brought to trial. I will testify on your behalf that you did the right thing by releasing the hostage."

"O'Malley must think I'm a real dunce," *The Weasel* said aloud. "I know the penalty for kidnapping and your testimony would be worthless," he said as he sneered at me, Then speaking into the phone, he responded, "You have a good point. She's getting to be a problem anyway. I will release her at the next rest stop and give her back her phone. She can call you with her location. If you double-cross me, all bets are off and you all know what that means."

It was reassuring to learn later that the rescue unit had the car under surveillance the whole time so they knew where I, in all probability, would be released. The police cruisers circled around and came to the appointed rest stop from another direction in order to arrive before *The Weasel* and find a spot where they could set up watch undetected. The helicopter was forced to stay back so as not to alert or spook *The Weasel* when he got out of his car. One of the features of *The Weasel's* new car was that it minimized outside noise when the windows were all up. Thus, he would have been unable to hear the roar of the helicopter even when in close proximity.

Upon reaching the rest area, *The Weasel* had me change into the clothes he had obtained at the warehouse, and in turn, placed

my clothing on the mannequin. He then positioned the mannequin at one of the picnic tables. He returned to the car and we
sped out of the rest area onto the highway passing every vehicle in sight. He said he wanted to put some miles between him
and the cops before they discovered his ruse. As I watched all of
this from the backseat of *The Weasel's* vehicle, my heart throbbed.
I was then ordered to scrunch down in the backseat and "disappear." *The Weasel* then advised me of what the consequences
would be if I didn't follow his every command. I was now sec-
ond-guessing my decision to wait for the ideal opportunity to
escape. I was beginning to feel that I had squandered my last
real opportunity back at the rest area. I had actually squandered
two opportunities: one was when *The Weasel* left me alone in the
car when he went inside the warehouse; the other at the rest
area when two teenage boys were playing catch with a Frisbee
within shouting distance. For the first time during the ordeal, I
broke down and cried uncontrollably. All then seemed hopeless.
At times I had whimpered and shed tears, but this time I cried
buckets. *The Weasel* turned around almost running off the side of
the road and threatened that if I continued he would stuff his fist
down my throat. I knew he would only give me one warning, so I
instantly muffled the sound—at least on the outside.

The police vehicles, I was later told, converged on the rest
stop and carefully approached the mannequin they believed to
be me. Tank's father called out my name but, when there was no
response, he and the other officers later said they immediately
sensed something was awry. When they were close enough and
discovered they were duped, they were beyond furious. Tank's
father got back on the cell phone knowing he needed to remain
in control so as not irritate *The Weasel* to the point that would
cause *The Weasel* to do something foolish. When *The Weasel* re-

sponded, Tank's father said, "Very clever. You won round one. Are you through playing games with us now? What do you propose? Putting you behind bars isn't worth trading the life of a precious child for the death penalty. Name your conditions and we will comply. All we want is the hostage released."

"Let me think about it. The battery on this cell phone is getting low so I'm turning it off to conserve what power is left. When I decide what I want, *I'll* contact *you*. I have your number stored in the phone. For now I strongly *suggest* you boys all go back to town and take that nuisance that has been circling overhead with you," answered *The Weasel*. He then said again loud enough for me to hear and maybe even mainly for my benefit, "What on earth could they think they have to offer? I have the bank money, I have a fast car and I have the advantage of a hostage. All I really want is to get to Mexico and then make my way to some country that doesn't have an extradition treaty with the U.S. Once I get to El Paso and cross over into Juarez, I will release you. If I drive all night, we can be in El Paso by mid-day."

The Weasel had no intention of letting the cops know his plans. He would not contact them again and he hoped by turning off the cell phone they would be unable to track him. Just to make sure, he tossed my cell phone out of the car window. I gasped as I watched my only contact with the outside world tumble across the shoulder of the road and disappear into the thick sage beyond. By now, as I said, I had given up on ever being rescued. Any escape opportunities I might have had, I was convinced, I had relinquished. I resolved that I wouldn't let *The Weasel* know how distraught I was—as if he didn't already know. I dried up all my tears and prayed more fervently than ever before.

The Weasel stopped at a convenience store and let me use the restroom but not without a lecture on what would happen to me and everyone in the store if I made a scene or any false move. When I came out, *The Weasel* checked the restroom to make sure I hadn't left a distress message of some sort for the next person who used the facility to see. Satisfied I had not, he ushered me back to the Passat and securely locked me in the backseat. He then went back inside the convenience store and purchased a maxi-sized container of black coffee for himself and some snacks and fruit drinks for me. He said it would be a long tedious trip and wasn't sure about the availability of fuel along the route, so he filled the gas tank to the brim and even purchased a gas can which he also filled with gasoline "just in case."

MEANWHILE, BACK IN JEFFERSON City, Tank's father, I learned later, had called a meeting of the SWAT team assigned to his division. Everyone was then briefed on the situation and began formulating a rescue plan. I was told the team studied a topographic map and speculated on which way *The Weasel* would travel. The possibilities to them were deemed limitless. However, at the end of the day, they, I was told, they collectively agreed that *The Weasel*, in all likelihood, would be heading for Mexico since *The Weasel* would figure that that would be the best way to avoid apprehension and extradition (being sent back to the U.S.).

Now, the problem the team faced, I later learned, was in trying to determine which border crossing *The Weasel* would choose. He was half-way between El Paso, which would be the gateway to Juarez, and Tucson, which would be the gateway to Nogales. What the team didn't know at the time was that *The Weasel* had spent some time in El Paso and was familiar with the area. His decision, therefore, was an easy one. He would use El Paso as the gateway into Mexico. I could hear him chuckle as he no doubt considered himself infallible.

The city police along with the SWAT team, fortunately, had determined it would be prudent to alert both the El Paso and Tucson border authorities of their suspicions. Accordingly, they provided the border authorities with a description and temporary license plate number of the Passat as well as descriptions of *The Weasel* and me. At the end of the meeting, Tank's father reputedly rubbed his chin and said, "Since we're not really sure of his destination, we may be wise to just issue an ABP (all-points bulletin) nationwide. He may be headed for Canada or maybe some desolate island. Who knows where or what other tricks *The Weasel* has up his sleeve. He is one slippery eel!"

"We don't really have a great margin for error. A young girl's life lies in the balance," Michael Blake, the SWAT team leader allegedly replied. "In the interim, I'll keep my team at the ready and the chopper primed. We are but two minutes from takeoff when we get the order."

Though battle ready, the authorities in reality were stymied in their rescue efforts. There were too many unknowns. They, too, were second guessing their strategy and were blaming themselves for having let *The Weasel* slip through their net. The only thing they could do now was wait and hope *The Weasel* would make a mistake. Tank's father instructed police personnel to issue the APB and then left for home. He hadn't slept for several days and said later he was beginning to feel the effects of fatigue. "Knowing what was at stake was taking its toll—not just on me but everyone else as well," he allegedly told Tank's mother.

CHAPTER THREE

WHEN ALL ELSE FAILS

t was obvious *The Weasel* was also feeling the effects of stress and the lack of sleep. He stopped several times to replenish his black coffee and stretch but it had begun to have little effect on him. I watched as he rubbed his eyes and yawned constantly. "I need to stay alert," he kept saying aloud. "I cannot afford to fall asleep. I'll get caught for sure and spend the rest of my life behind bars. Maybe just five minutes at the next rest stop..." I was now concerned that he might doze off and cause a serious accident. I wasn't ready to die—not then and maybe never.

Because of his exhausted state, *The Weasel* had difficulty concentrating on the road signs and it wasn't long before he missed a turnoff. When he discovered his mistake, he tried to compensate by taking a short cut down a country road. It had rained that afternoon and the road was muddy and in disrepair. We jostled along in the deep ruts. Soon *The Weasel* encountered a creek that ran parallel to the road that had over-flowed and spilled over onto the road. The spillage didn't appear to be very deep or extensive. So, *The Weasel* attempted to forge across. The wheels began spinning but the car stayed in one spot. I cringed as he kept gunning the engine trying to steer the car through the muddy mass until he realized it was of no avail. Unbeknownst to us, the car had become high centered on a boulder lurking under the murky creek water. A good or a bad omen, at the time, I didn't know. I just surmised it would delay the inevitable.

The Weasel desperately tried to rock the car free without success. The rocking motion, as it turned out, created a large hole in the oil pan of the car and immediately the oil began leaking out and the surface of the water around us blackened. *The Weasel* got out of the car and tried to push it free. Not only was he unable to budge it but his efforts only resulted in getting himself wet, cold and covered with slimy mud and oil slick. He banged his fists against the trunk in frustration, raving and cursing as was his custom. Since he was already wet and covered with mud and oil, he got down on his hands and knees to see how badly the car was high-centered. It was then that he apparently realized our true predicament. This seemed to infuriate him even more. After a few hectic moments of stomping around, waving his arms and cursing, *The Weasel* finally calmed down. He repeated over and over again that he was a survivor and he would overcome this obstacle. He got back into the car and that was where we spent the night.

The sun was peeking over the horizon when *The Weasel* awakened me. He instructed me to "stay put." He stepped out into the muddy creek and tried again to free the car. It was then we noticed some smoke curling in the distance. He said it looked like it was coming from a chimney which meant there was a house close by. He untied me and helped me out of the backseat. He hung onto my hand as I waded through water and mud that came up past my knees. *The Weasel* reminded me that we both were in a survival mode and dependent upon each other, and therefore, should look out for each other. He then led me in the direction of where the smoke was rising, and again cautioned me to keep my silence should we encounter the occupants. "If you alert or attempt to alert anyone even in the slightest, I'll know and all of you will be sorry!" he said to me in a gruff voice. I knew he meant business and with the reprieve began a new hope for escape. So, the journey in mutual preservation began and I pretended to be content with the predicament.

THE SMOKE WAS INDEED coming from a farmhouse. In fact, a picture perfect storybook farmhouse which was situated in the middle of a very well kept farm. Fields of corn surrounded the house which boasted a beautiful white wrap-around porch sporting an inviting swing and two white wicker rocking chairs padded with colorful flower print pillows. There was an expanse of manicured lawn with assorted flower beds scattered throughout including a variety of blooming rose bushes enhancing the total fairytale scene. It was truly an oasis. It reminded me of my own home back in Jefferson City. The farmhouse in its setting was most inviting and I had to again fight back the tears that welled in my eyes. I so missed my home, my loving parents, the R*U*1*2s, and most of all Genius and Tank. I had already missed the first day of school and hoped my absence would be temporary and not permanent. Yes, I was starting to doubt whether I would ever be liberated and fought the urge to just let nature take its course.

As we approached the farmhouse, *The Weasel* glared at me and squeezed my arm until it hurt. There was an unspoken threat in the gesture and I shuddered under the spell of his touch. With me in tow, he walked boldly up to the front door and knocked. After a few seconds, a kindly middle-aged woman answered. "Yah, what is it I can do for ya?" She said with a Norwegian accent. She was a rather large matronly-looking woman. Her blonde hair, somewhat graying at the temples, was braided and wrapped around her head making a halo atop rosy cheeks, piercing blue eyes and a pink smiling mouth.

I was instantly drawn to the woman and sensed the woman's maternal instinct, comfort and help. "Wouldja just look at yourselves now. You be all muddy and the little one looks hungry. Take off them muddy shoes and come in, ya," she said taking me by the hand. "Ya, you're cold, little one, go to the fire and warm yourself while I find some dry coveralls for the mister." I entered the pleasant foyer and looked around. I had seen pictures in magazines of paintings by Norman Rockwell, a great American artist, and the interior, as well as the exterior, of the farmhouse was typical "Rockwell." Rockwell's paintings depicted Americans going about their everyday life and were so lifelike they could have been photographs.

I detected what smelled like cinnamon-flavored apple pie baking in the warm kitchen as I entered and walked to the fireplace. A kettle of steaming water was suspended on a hook over the open flame and was making gurgling sounds reminiscent of a percolating pot of tea, only with more gusto. The warmth of the fire felt good and inviting. I was beginning to feel a little more hopeful that there might be a tomorrow on the horizon after all.

The Weasel remained on the porch at the woman's bidding until he could change into the coveralls she was "fetching" for him. When she returned, he went to the side of the house and quickly changed. He used the garden hose to rinse the mud and sludge from his clothes and his and my shoes and placed them on the porch railing to dry. Then, after he was allowed to enter, he quickly looked at me in an effort obviously to determine if I had said anything that would expose his charade. Everything must have seemed "normal" and he seemed to relax believing thus far his secret had remained intact.

"I'm Ada Knudsen and I ask what brings the two of ya to these parts?"

"Oh, ah, we got lost and then we tried to backtrack by taking a shortcut on the county road out yonder." *The* Weasel then pointed in the direction of the abandoned vehicle. "We got stuck in the mud and high-centered our vehicle. I think I'll need help getting it out of the mud and towed into town to be repaired."

"Yah, probably so. The mister will soon be in from the chores for his morning break and can pull ya out with his tractor. Of that, I am certain. Would you like a snack and hot tea while ya wait?" Ada asked as she looked lovingly at me.

"Yah, oh, sorry, I mean yes," I said. Despite Ada's accent, I was able to understand her.

Ada smiled pleasantly at me and began preparing a plate of homemade pastries for both *The Weasel* and me. She then asked, "Is pretty girl your daughter?"

"What? Ah, no, she's, ah, ah, my niece. I'm taking her to California for a visit with her two cousins."

"Humm, seems odd. Thought school already started." Then turning to me, she asked, "Are you going to school in California, child?"

Before I could answer, *The Weasel* interrupted, "No. Ah, umm, you see, she's handicapped mentally. She attends a 'special ed' school and it will not start for another two weeks."

I stared dagger's at *The Weasel* giving new dimension to the term "If looks could kill."

Ada, I hoped, was not so easily fooled. It wasn't until later that I learned she sensed something was not right and was convinced when she saw the rope burns on my wrists. She looked at me and said, "Sit, child, and eat. Can I bring ya a glass of milk?"

Before *The Weasel* could answer for me, I said, "Thank you, I would like that."

As soon as we finished our snack, Knute Knudsen came in the back door. He was hot and sweaty from his morning chores. "Yah, what have we here?" he asked as he took off his hat and unfastened his coveralls. Before Ada could respond, he held out his hand and introduced his wife and himself. "This is Ada," he said. "I'm Lars Knudsen but everyone in these parts just calls me Knute." As he shook Knute's hand, *The Weasel* said, "I'm Wilber Smith and this is my, ah, err, niece, Jessica. She has a learning disability, you know." Knute looked at me with sympathetic eyes and shook his head. I just raised my eyebrows and managed a smile.

"They are having car problems and are stuck in the road down yonder," Ada interjected pointing in the direction of the swollen creek where it crossed the road.

"Yah. Old John Deere tractor pull ya out. No worry. Now I eat pastries Ada fix. She good baker."

SINCE THERE WAS ONLY room for two on the tractor that meant that I would be staying behind with Ada. *The Weasel* gave me a threatening look as if to say, *You better keep quiet or else.* I still didn't know what to expect and once again withered from his gaze. Out of the corner of my eye, I could see Ada bite her lower lip and look down as she fumbled with the hem of her apron. It was obvious she was a caring, sensitive woman and I suspected she realized something was amiss. When the men left, I helped Ada clean up the kitchen and start dinner. Then I curled up on the brightly colored braided oval rug in front of the fireplace, at Ada's coaxing, and dozed off. I hadn't had any restful sleep since I was kidnapped and was physically, emotionally and mentally exhausted—especially after spending a night in a cramped car high-centered in a swollen stream.

After a couple of hours, the men returned. *The Weasel* looked about obviously trying to determine if I had said anything. He seemed satisfied when he saw me rubbing sleep from my eyes as he entered the front room.

"Well, we got car out but much damage underneath. Car mess. Needs good wash. Car will have to be taken to town for repair. We go first thing tomorrow. No mechanic on duty today. Stanley's day off. I can pull car with truck to mechanic, yah. We will put Mr. Smith and Jessica up for the night," he said to Ada. Tuning to me he said, "Have guest rooms for the two of ya." To *The Weasel*, he said, "You help with chores, I help clean car."

The Weasel insisted I be outside with him and Knute as they cleaned the Passat inside and outside. It was obvious he wanted me to spend as little time alone with Ada as possible. It was lunch time before the chores were completed. The rest of the day was spent working on the Passat.

After dinner, which included the apple pie I had smelled when we first entered the farm house, Ada began preparing sleeping arrangements. She was going to put me in one room and *The Weasel* in another.

"Oh, no, no. That will never do," *The Weasel* said, "Sha…, I mean Jessica, is prone to having nightmares and gets scared in strange places. Just set out a mattress on the floor in my room where I can calm her if she gets frightened."

Ada looked at me with a puzzled look on her face. She would later say she had not detected any mental problems during the time she spent with me and was getting even more suspicious. She did, however, comply with *The Weasel's* "request." After breakfast, the next morning, when Knute, *The Weasel* and I were getting ready for the trip to town, Ada suddenly remembered she needed some groceries.

"Wait. I write a list for you." Ada wrote a few grocery items on the list and then at the bottom she wrote: "If you're in trouble, blink at me." She gave the list to me. "Ah, you look at list. Make sure you can read." She then waited. I read the list and the notation at the bottom. I jerked my head up, and looking directly at Ada while *The Weasel* was distracted in conversation with Knute, I blinked my eyes. Then, not sure she got the signal, did it for a second time. This time I exaggerated the blink hoping she got the drift.

"Come on, come on. We're wasting time." *The Weasel* commanded. I had made sure *The Weasel* would be unable to detect the interchange between Ada and me. And thankfully, it appeared he hadn't. Ada then asked for the note she gave me back. She said she didn't need one of the items after all. She then tore off the bottom part of the list containing the notation and handed the part that just listed the grocery items back. *The Weasel* peered at the part Ada had handed back, folded it and put it in his pants pocket. "Wow! That was close," I thought. As far as I know, neither Ada nor I flinched.

The three of us climbed into Knute's old faded green Ford truck, and with the Passat in tow, headed for what Knute said was the nearest town. As soon as we left, Ada, I later learned, was on the phone to the Chief of Police. She explained the situation and requested the Chief to at least question "Mr. Smith." Chief Perry Blanton apparently agreed to do so. He then left his office and went to the place of business of the only mechanic shop in town, Olvson's Machine Works, to await the arrival of Knute and the "strangers."

Glenville was a small quiet town. There were only two peace officers employed, the Chief and one patrol officer. A few minutes before we arrived, the Chief was paged by the patrol officer to come immediately to his location. There apparently had been a bad accident on the highway on the other side of town and the injured driver was in need of medical attention. Chief Blanton later said he had no choice but to respond. He said he hurriedly left the garage and headed in the direction to where the accident had occurred. My plight now hung in the balance, and through no one's fault, Chief Blanton's attention would be diverted and he would not be available to intercede.

When Knute pulled into the garage area, only the mechanic, Stanley Webber, who was now on duty, was present. Stanley was a sluggish man who really didn't notice much going on about him; a man who kept pretty much to himself. The Chief later said he had not said anything to Stanley about Ada's call because "there was no evidence of foul play only Ada's unsubstantiated supposition." "The Knudsen woman had a reputation of cry-ing wolf-wolf," he would later say. "So, I didn't give her concerns much credence."

Wiping his greasy hands on a rag, Stanley greeted us and asked what he could do for us. When *The Weasel* explained the situation, Stanley put the Passat on the rack and raised it so he could examine the undercarriage. "Sure 'nuf," he stated, "looks like the oil pan is ruined and will need to be replaced."

"Do you have any parts for this model?" *The Weasel* asked.

"Nope, have to have them brought over from Jensen. I can get them delivered this afternoon. As soon as they get here, it will only take about an hour or so to do the work. If you want me to replace the oil pan, I'll have to make the call right away. They start their deliveries around ten, ten-thirty."

"Doesn't look like I have a choice. Get with it!" *The Weasel* barked.

Stanley spat out his tobacco and sauntered over to the phone and placed the call after which he turned to *The Weasel* and said, "You're in luck, Mister. They were just getting ready to leave. They have the parts and can deliver them this afternoon."

Knute suggested that they go back to the farm and have Stanley call when the car was repaired. *The Weasel* rolled his eyes, obviously in disgust. How much more was he going to have to endure before reaching Mexico—his safe haven, he must have thought. I heard him mutter, "Now we have to spend another day with the hicks."

When we returned to the farmhouse, Ada seemed surprised. I suspect she was sure the Chief would have discovered whatever secret we were harboring and have placed Wilber Smith under arrest. Ada was not a very good actress and had trouble disguising her dislike for *The Weasel*. I prayed she would not show her true feelings or do something that would evoke *The Weasel's* ire. I was not as much concerned about myself as I was about Ada and Kunte. The Knudsens were innocent bystanders and I didn't want them harmed.

The Weasel was a crafty creature and I was fairly certain he realized Ada was onto his tricks. Ada went about preparing lunch with my help. There was no opportunity to question me as *The Weasel* was constantly present and keeping a watchful eye on me. I did not want to cause trouble for the Knudsens, as I previously said, so I played along maintaining a cheerful attitude careful not to upset *The Weasel*. I knew *The Weasel* had a short fuse.

The afternoon passed by all too slowly. I wasn't sure if Knute was aware of the tension. If he was, he showed no reaction. Ada didn't have an opportunity, as far as I could determine, to pull her husband aside and express her concerns. Ada, when later interviewed by the authorities, said she felt Knute, in all likelihood would do something rash and get them all in hot water if she was to have said anything. She said she detected the "killer instinct" in "Mr. Smith." She could see it in his eyes, she said. The Police Chief, it later turned out, was correct when he surmised that Ada had a tendency to overreact and "make a mountain out of a mole hill." Consequently, when a real emergency arose, such as now, no one was inclined to put much faith in Ada's purported intuition. This, of course, had not worked to my benefit.

Finally the telephone rang, and Knute answered on the second ring. "Yah, you have car fixed. Goot. We will be there right quick." Turning to *The Weasel*, Knute said, "We should leave now. Garage closes at five. We hurry." He didn't have to ask *The Weasel* twice. *The Weasel*, obviously, was more than ready. *The Weasel* said to Ada, as he reached for my hand and started for the door, "Your kindness is appreciated. We won't be coming back to the house. We have lost enough valuable time as it is and need to be getting on down the road."

I broke loose from *The Weasel's* grasp and ran back to Ada and gave her a big hug. I looked up into the kind woman's face, and out of the eyeshot of *The Weasel*, blinked three times in quick succession. She raised her eyebrows and cringed. She held onto my hands with both of hers and squeezed them. *The Weasel* had to pull me away.

The Weasel's face flushed and he shook with anger. He ordered me to go ahead, he would be right behind me. After I went outside, *The Weasel* had words with Ada. I was out of earshot but later learned he had said to Ada, "If you do anything foolish, I mean anything, I won't hesitate harming you, the girl and Knute. DO YOU UNDERSTAND?" He then exited the farmhouse and caught up to Knute and me.

As *The Weasel* joined Knute and me in the truck, Ada appeared in the doorway and waved goodbye. Tears rolled down my face as I returned the wave sensing that Ada had been threatened by *The Weasel* and watched as she dabbed at tears from her eyes with the edge of her apron and walked back inside the farmhouse.

I WOULD LATER LEARN that the Knudsens were friendly with their neighbors and the couples often took turns having each other over for dinner. Ada, I was later told, decided to call Olsa Swenson, her closest neighbor, and seek her advice and assistance. Hagar and Olsa Swenson were also from Norway and shared the Knudsens' support for the Nordic Ski Alliance (NSA). They had much in common and did some share-cropping together. They were, without question, folks Ada could trust.

When Ada called the Swenson residence, there was no answer. She later said, this distressed her even more. Finally, she said she decided to call the Chief of Police again. Chief Blanton answered on the first ring. He had just finished his accident report and was preparing to go home for a well-deserved rest and hot meal. When Chief Blanton answered, Ada pleaded, "Chief, dat young child in some terrible situation with that Smith guy. She tell me dat. Something ornery and evil about him. He threatened me. I fear for young child. She need your help. They now with my mister in truck going Olvson's Machine Works garage to get fixed car. Please make sure she okay." Chief Blanton said he decided it wouldn't take all that much time to run over to the garage and check out Ada's fears. If the girl was in "trouble," he later said he would be remiss in his duties as Chief of Police to "poo-poo" it so he put on his hat and headed in the direction of Olvson's Machine Works.

When the Chief entered the garage, he said, *The Weasel's* Passat was still on the rack. He said he asked Stanley where everyone was. Stanley apparently replied, "Welp, you see, Chief, I hit a snag when I lowered the rack. I didn't notice the dolly was still under the car and I lowered the rack right on top of it flattening the left front tire—the accident didn't help the dolly much either, she was clean destroyed. Smith didn't have a spare because of some previous tire trouble so Knute took him and the girl and they headed to the tire shop to get a replacement. He surely wasn't a happy camper. I've never seen anyone have a fit like that over a flat tire. Offered to pay for it but he went on-and-on ranting and cursing like you wouldn't believe. Offered to watch the girl while they went but he weren't havin' any part of that either." The Chief scratched his head, and later said, his interest was piqued. *Maybe Ada was onto something after all.* "Thanks Stanley," he said. "Think I'll go on over to the tire shop and do some checking."

THE WEASEL WAS MAKING his tire selection when Chief Blanton arrived. Upon seeing the Chief, *The Weasel* grabbed me by the arm and whispered, "Don't do anything stupid!" It was obvious *The Weasel* was nervous upon catching sight of the uniformed officer.

"Lo, Chief," Knute said.

"Howdy, Knute. Ya gonna introduce me to your friends here?"

"Shore nuf', this here is Mr. Smith and his niece, Jessica. They had some car trouble yesterday after the rain and me and the misses have been helpin' 'em out."

Sticking out his hand toward *The Weasel*, Chief Blanton said, "Glad to make your 'quintance. You folks hale from 'round here?"

The Weasel appeared stilted and ruffled upon coming face-to-face with a law officer after all the trauma he'd been through the past several days. He, however, regained his composure somewhat and cordially greeted the Chief and then shook his hand. "No, sir, we're not from these parts. We're just passing through on our way to California where my niece is going to spend the school year with her cousin. Her mom thought it would be a good experience for her to go to a different school. Lord knows those Californians *are* a different breed."

"Ummhumm. Just 'zactly where you from anyway?" the Chief asked raising his eyebrows.

"Why?" *The Weasel* asked with a sneer in his patented weaselistic manner reminiscent of bygone days. "We under arrest or something?"

"Naw, just curious, that's all. Hey, little lady, you ain't had much to say. What did they say your name was?"

Before I could answer, *The Weasel* stepped between the Chief and me and said, "Her name is Jessica. She is rather bashful and don't talk much." With that *The Weasel* gave me a glare that translated into "You better keep your trap shut or else."

"Humm, she just don't look like the shy type. Mind if I talk directly to her?"

The Weasel didn't have any choice but to agree. He stepped aside and the Chief took me by the hand and started to lead me away.

"HOLD ON THERE, PARTNER," *The Weasel* shouted. "I said you could talk to her, not take her off somewhere."

"Relax, buddy. I'm the Chief of Police. She couldn't be in any safer hands. I'm just going to take her across the street for ice cream and have a friendly chat. Lost my daughter when she was about Jessica's age. In fact, Jessica reminds me of Rayette. Hopefully, you don't mind."

Controlling his anger, *The Weasel* said he didn't and watched as the Chief and I walked hand-in-hand toward the exit.

Knute, taking all of this in, later said he was somewhat dumbfounded as to why the Chief of Police might want to talk to me and why "Mr. Smith" acted the way he did. Knute didn't have Ada's insight and obviously did not know what was in Ada's mind. *The Weasel* finished the tire purchase. He purchased two in order to have a spare. When he pulled the wad of cash out of his pocket, Knute said his eyes got big with wonder but he politely said nothing. The two men wheeled the tires out to Knute's truck and loaded them into the back. Knute suggested they take them to Olvson's Machine Works—which was just around the corner and have the Chief bring Jessica there. Knute later admitted he was getting anxious to be rid of the stranger and was beginning to have suspicions of his own.

CHIEF BLANTON LED ME to the Glenville Confectionary across the street from Olvson's Machine Works. We ordered strawberry ice cream sodas and sat outside on the log-hewn benches. The Chief chose his words carefully. Frowning, he finally said, "Tell me, is Smith really your uncle?"

"No," I replied without any hesitation.

"What are you doing with him?" the Chief asked. Again, his eyes narrowed.

"He kidnapped me," I replied looking around to make sure we were not overheard.

"WHAT! Do you realize what you are saying?"

"Yes. He said he would hurt me and my family if I told anyone. I think he's the one who robbed the bank in Jefferson City, Iowa, a few days ago. I was playing with some friends and next thing I knew I was grabbed and thrown into the backseat of his car. He took me to a shack in the oilfield where he blindfolded me and tied me up. We stayed there for a couple of days. When we left, we were chased by the police but he managed to get away using me as a hostage. My daddy works for the police."

Placing the palm of his left hand to his forehead and his right hand on the holster strap of his service revolver, the Chief said, "I knew something wasn't quite right. You stay right here, Little Lady. I'm going to have another chat with our 'Mr. Smith.'" The Chief ushered me inside the confectionary with instructions to stay out of sight. He told the proprietor to stand guard until he returned. The Chief then walked back across the street in the direction of Olvson's Machine Woks. By then, I was pulled out of sight.

The Weasel apparently had started to exit Olvson's Machine Works, and spotting the Chief marching his way, stopped in his tracks. He, no doubt, surmised I had told the Chief about being kidnapped. At any rate, he didn't wait around to see what was going to happen next. He, according to the Chief, turned and fled back inside Olvson's Machine Works. I was told later *The* Weasel had grabbed the car keys from Stanley. He jumped in the Passat and sped off through the open bay door as fast as he could. Stanley and Knute, later related that they stood in disbelief watching as gravel was spewed in the wake of *The Weasel's* rapid departure. The Chief was some distance away from his patrol car and it took him several minutes to retrace his steps. He said he was positive he couldn't catch "the fleeing felon." He said he was miserably outclassed by the new Passat. He stopped long enough on his way past Glenville Confectionary to tell me he was taking me with him. He loaded me in the patrol car with me holding on for dear life to my unfinished ice cream soda. I wasn't about to relinquish my first real treat in quite a spell. We headed straight to the Glenville police department.

Once inside, Chief Blanton immediately broadcast an APB on *The Weasel.* He gave a description of the car and its license number which he had noted earlier. After he had taken care of alerting other law enforcement agencies and getting them involved in the pursuit, he obtained the telephone number for the Chief of Police in Jefferson City and made a call. He related to the Jefferson City Police Chief the events that had led up to his call. He said he could hear relief in the Chief's voice when he was told that I was safe. Chief Evans told Chief Blanton that he would make the appropriate phone calls and see that I was returned safe and sound to my parents. In the interim, Chief Blanton promised he would not let me out of his sight. He told Chief

Evans that he had broadcast the APB and felt certain that Mr. Smith or whoever he really was would soon be in custody.

Chief Blanton later would say he underestimated *The Weasel's* cunning and tenacity. On the trips to town with Knute, *The Weasel* had apparently scoped out several side roads that were not well traveled. When he left the garage, it was later learned, instead of heading to the interstate, he veered off onto one of the less traveled side roads. *The* Weasel would later say he didn't know where it went but he was sure it was a better choice than the heavily traveled interstate. *The Weasel* later admitted he was beyond angry. He said he was livid that I would *betray him*. He said it was then he made a vow to himself that he would some-day get even with me for exposing him to the ordeal he felt he would soon be facing.

The Weasel said he raged and swore as he bumped along the badly maintained twisty wash-board dirt road. The road apparently led past several well-kept farms and one dairy. After about forty-five minutes, *The Weasel* said he came to an intersection. The signs indicated that he could turn left and intersect with Interstate Highway 10, which would take him to Houston, or he could turn right and follow Interstate Highway 10 out of Texas into New Mexico, through Arizona and eventually to California. He said he chose the route to the right. The road signs proved to be bullet riddled thus obliterating the specified distances and even the names of some of the towns/cities so he said he just gritted his teeth and held on tightly to the steering wheel as he tore recklessly down the rough road.

It was now beginning to get dark and the gas gauge on *The Weasel's* Passat was nudging toward the empty mark when he said he saw that traffic had picked up and there were lights in the distance indicating that he was approaching a more populated area. After a few miles, he said he saw that he was on the outskirts of a small town which offered "Food and Gas" at the next exit. He took the exit and wheeled into the first gas station he saw. He filled up the tank and spare gas can and went inside where out of habit he purchased two sandwiches and two large cold drinks. He did not tarry or delay, according to his recollection, during this stop as he was anxious to distance himself from the area as far as he could and so he ate and drank as he drove.

The Weasel went past a used car dealership as his journey took him toward the other side of the small town and he decided that trading vehicles would be wise considering that his cover had been exposed and that the Passat "stuck out like a sore thumb." Luckily, he said, a salesman was just preparing to close for the day. He said he jerked to a stop in front of the small office and asked the salesman if he would assist him. He told the salesman that he wanted to trade his Passat for a pickup truck. He explained that his cousin had bought him the Passat and that the car was not suitable for his line of work which was, of course, farming. The salesman, when interviewed, later related that, sensing a quick deal, he readily agreed to help *The Weasel.*

There were several pickup trucks on the lot so *The Weasel* said he selected a non-descript blue and white older model Chevrolet and offered to trade straight across telling the salesman he was in a hurry and "didn't have time to haggle." The salesman, he said, was delighted to accommodate him and soon the deal was consummated and *The Weasel* was off and running once again, only this time in a vehicle that would not attract attention. I can just picture the salesman returning to the office shaking his head and thinking to himself, "That man must be an imbecile to trade a brand new Volkswagen Passat straight across for an older model Chevy pickup." But, then again, who was he to complain, he would boast. *Easy money is not an everyday occurrence.*

CHIEF EVANS CONTACTED TANK'S father who, in turn, contacted my parents advising them that I had been rescued and was safe at the police department in Glenville, Kansas. Upon hearing the news, my mother said she was so ecstatic that she laughed and cried both at the same time. It didn't take my parents long to make the trip from Jefferson City to Glenville to pick me up. In fact, Chief Evans had transported them in his police cruiser, sometimes with the lights flashing and the siren blaring in order to hasten the trip. When we were reunited, we hugged and held each other close and didn't want to let go. It was not long before we were invigorated by the realization that the nightmare was finally over and that I had been released safe and sound. The touching and closeness was all the confirmation that we needed to know that our prayers had been answered and that my release was no longer a dream but a reality. I still consider it a miracle.

"WHEN THE WEASEL HAD left in such a hurry without any explanation," Knute, would later say, "I was dumbfounded that an uncle would abandon his niece after being so overly protective of her the whole time they spent in Glenville." He said, "I just climbed back into my truck and headed for home." Once he arrived, he said he told Ada about the happenings. Ada, according to him, puffed up and said, "Vell, I knew all vas not right. I be the one who called police!" Knute, conceded that Ada was the hero of the day and my savior. Knute didn't have to convince me of Ada's role, and at the time, I didn't know how I would ever repay Ada for her determination. I just knew someday I would. The following summer, my parents and I visited Ada and Knute and gave them a $25,000.00 gift certificate to the John Deere Dealership.

Stanley, on the other hand, was left holding the bag so to speak because *The Weasel* had left without paying for the repairs to the Passat. Stanley knew there wouldn't be much left of his paycheck when his boss deducted *The Weasel's* long list of unpaid charges. After we left Ada and Knute with the gift certificate, we stopped in Glenville and left an envelope with five crisp $100 bills at Stanley's place of employment with his boss. Unfortunately, we could not thank Stanley in person because he had quit his job and moved out of town.

Sorry for the commentary. It's just that when I look back on that *one frightful day* and the days that followed, I never figured I would be alive long enough to recount the events. As you can see, I have a lot of people to thank. If it weren't for them, I wouldn't be here today to tell about it.

RETURNING TO THE STORY, I later learned that *The Weasel* had been plagued with lack of sleep. Fatigue and worry, he would later reveal, had become his constant companions. Having swapped vehicles, he said he decided he could safely pull into a rest stop and sleep for a couple of hours since the police, he presumed, had no clue that he was now driving a pickup. He found a rest stop a few miles out of town and pulled in. He said later he was dead tired and instantly fell asleep. Passing traffic apparently did not bother him, and it's been told, he slept for untold hours.

Upon awakening, *The Weasel* reputedly used the rest stop facilities to freshen up, splashing cold water on his face and washing the grime from his hands after which he got back into the truck and proceeded west on Interstate Highway 10. He said he knew that it would eventually lead him into El Paso if he kept on this route. El Paso was his destination because there, he would say, he could cross the border into Mexico where he felt he would be safe. He said he hoped he could make the crossing before the authorities discovered he had traded the Passat for a pickup and had obtained the description of the truck from the dealer. *The Weasel's* anxiety was quickly evolving into what the authorities later termed "relentless frenzy."

MEANWHILE, BACK IN JEFFERSON City, grammar school had already began. Kindergarten, however, had started a day earlier in order to give the new-comers an opportunity to acquaint themselves with the school and each other. Our favorite R*U*1*2, Rhymin' Sally Pearson, was just barely old enough to start kindergarten. She, it is told, was very excited because all the other *R*U*1*2s*, who were older, were already attending school. The community had an unexpected number of kindergartners for the current term and the school room was "bulging at the seams" and not adequately equipped to accommodate all of them. Supposedly, when Sally and her mother showed up a trifle late, the teacher, Ms. Hollenbeck, looked around the room and scratched her head. There apparently wasn't a desk for Sally. The teacher reputedly said to Sally, "You sit here for the *present* and just wait for a while," pointing to a chair positioned under one of the windows. "I'll have the custodian roundup some extra desks." Sally would later say she was elated when she took her seat on the chair. She said she could hardly wait for the promised *present* and a desk of her very own.

At the end of the school day when Sally's mother picked her up, her mother said she noticed Sally was sad and quiet. She then asked Sally what was wrong. Sally apparently said,

> *Mommy, my teacher told me 'for the present sit here.'*
> *I'm sure I heard her loud and clear.*
> *So I sat on the chair and did so with care.*
> *I thought doing as I was told was as good as gold.*
> *I waited and wondered what the present would be.*
> *But at the end of the day no present did I see.*
> *What do you think, Mommy, did she lie?*
> *I'm so disappointed, I could cry."*

Sally's mother said she wasn't sure she could control herself. She didn't know whether to laugh or cry. She said she gathered Sally in her arms and gave her a big "mommy hug." She said she then explained that there was no *present* or gift as such. She told Sally that the teacher had meant for Sally to sit on the chair for the time being or as the teacher put it "the present" until the custodian could bring her a desk. Oh," said Sally as the last tear fell from her eye,

> *Can we get an ice cream cone instead?*
> *Then school I will no longer dread.*

"Yes, Sally, you deserve a treat," her mother allegedly replied. And with that, her mother said, they headed to Dairy Treat and didn't miss a beat. Sally had made it through her first day of school and her ABCs and her rhyming ways would become her legacy. I know this has little to do with our story, but Sally was and still is a big part of my R*U*1*2 story. I think the incident deserved to be told. I hope you don't think me bold. With Sally, they threw away the mold.

AFTER MY RESCUE AND reunification with my parents, we were driven back to Jefferson City by Chief Evans. We arrived home at the close of the school day. I immediately telephoned Genius to let him know I was home and safe and sound. He said he was so excited to hear my voice that he could scarcely talk—a rarity for Genius. I found it difficult back then, as well as today, to talk to Genius about the ordeal without becoming emotional. All of us were grateful the nightmare was finally over. School had started a few days earlier but I found that I had not missed much. Genius told me he would bring me up to speed the next day and offered to walk me to school so we could visit before classes started. After our brief conversation, I fell asleep with excited expectancy. I was anxious for the morrow. I could hardly wait to see Genius, Tank, my classmates, and needless to say, my fellow *R*U*1*2s*.

The next morning, Genius arrived at my house as prearranged. We shared a hug and I bid my parents a fond good-bye before we left for school. Mother was reluctant to let me leave her sight because of the nightmare of the previous week but she knew she could not keep me isolated forever so she grudgingly let me go. As we walked along, Genius reached into his pocket and pulled out a small wrapped box tied with a pink ribbon and handed it to me. "For me?" I asked.

"Go ahead and open it." Genius insisted.

"Okay, but what is it?" I asked.

"There's only one way to find out," Genius replied.

With that, I pulled the ribbon free from the box and let the ribbon flutter to the sidewalk. I did the same with the fancy wrapper. I hesitated a brief moment and looked into Genius' eyes. They sparkled and his broad smile told me that what was inside the box was something special.

"Well…" he said and pointed to the box.

I lifted the lid and peered inside. Inside was a shiny new sterling silver charm bracelet that glistened in the morning sun. It was exactly like the one that I had lost when I was kidnapped except there was another charm added to the cat, bicycle, heart and star. It was a small silver cross with a small diamond in the center. It's beautiful," I said.

"I knew God would protect you and that you would come home safe. The cross is to signify our faith in a loving, gracious and merciful God." Genius then tenderly fastened the bracelet around my wrist where it would become a sacred talisman and a lasting reminder of our special friendship. By the way, when the bracelet found at the scene of my abduction was no longer needed as evidence in *The Weasel's* case, it was returned to me by the authorities. The old bracelet continues to be a reminder of the fragile nature of life, and the new bracelet? A reminder that there is always a pot of gold at the end of every rainbow; bright light after every dark night; and opportunity after we think all the doors have been closed.

"Thank you, not only for the bracelet but for your prayers and friendship." I told Genius, "I was broken hearted at losing the first bracelet but this one is even sweeter." I then took Genius' hand and gave it a gentle squeeze transmitting, I'm afraid, a bit more than just friendship. He reciprocated with a gentle squeeze of his own. The ordeal had solidified our bond, a bond that endures to this day.

After school my first day back, the *R*U*1*2s* gathered at the clubhouse and swarmed around me expressing their joy and gratitude at having me back among them. In short order, Rhymin'

Sally crawled up on my lap and put her arms around my neck. She whispered in my ear:

> *Oh, Shacoo, we were very concerned*
> *And are glad you've returned.*
> *We met and prayed each and every day*
> *That God would help you find the way.*
> *Now our wish has come true*
> *And we're thankful no harm has come to you.*

As you can imagine, I was choked with emotion. I couldn't say anything so I just gave Sally a big hug back. I found Sally to be a concerned and caring friend. Sally's rhyming would no longer be an impediment to our friendship. I just hoped it wasn't contagious.

Things returned to a semblance of normality as fall quickly passed into winter and Christmas loomed around the corner. The public was still on the alert for *The Weasel* but despite his elusiveness and his unpredictability, the odds were he would never pass this way again.

CHAPTER FOUR

HOME FOR THE HOLIDAYS

ittle did we know at the time that *The Weasel* was growing tired of Mexico and his self-imposed exile. It was only later that we learned he was homesick for the states and decided that enough time had passed and that it would be safe to return to Jefferson City. He had better than normal computer skills that he had acquired during his incarceration in the various detention facilities around the country. He bought a cheap computer and busied himself with the task of creating a new identity.

One of *The Weasel's* cellmates, Mitch Altman, was imprisoned on forgery charges and computer fraud and was looking at a long stint in the slammer. Mitch was more than eager to share his expertise with his fellow inmates. His mantra was, "The more, the merrier." *The Weasel* was a fast learner and recognized the value of being able to forge fake documents for use in the outside world. He soon learned the skills associated with deceiving the public at large—one of his favorite pastimes. He reveled in deception and was becoming proficient at it. He was smug in the belief that he would never again be caught. His humility was exceeded only by his brilliance, or so he would brag.

As *The Weasel* feverishly poured over the computer creating a new birth certificate, high school diploma, driver's license, social security card, passport and letters of recommendation from imaginary employers, he chuckled to himself. *How very easy it was to fool all the people all the time.* He still had the truck for which he had traded his Passat before leaving the states but knew keeping it, in all likelihood, would ultimately lead to his inevitable detection and ultimate arrest. He approached Manuel Trujillo, the owner of the inn at which *The Weasel* was staying while still in Mexico, with an offer. Manuel had a very nice looking older truck that had apparently been "babied" all its life because it was in such pristine condition. *The Weasel* still had plenty of money left from the bank robbery so, it is told, he offered Manuel $2,000 and his truck in trade for Manuel's truck. Manuel, apparently shaking his head from side to side and scratching his chin, stated in broken English, "Not sure. Plenty good truck. Don't know if I want to part with 'er."

Irritated, *The Weasel* apparently upped the offer of the trade; his truck and $2,500 for Manuel's.

"No, Senior. It's not the offer. I just don't wanna part with 'er. She's like a baby. We been through a lot together."

"OKAY! My last offer is $3,000. Take it or leave it!" With that *The Weasel* said he segregated thirty $100 bills from a wad in his front pocket and fanned it in front of Manuel.

Manuel's eyes, *The Weasel* would later boast, got big as poker chips at the sight of the green stuff and he finally relented. "Okay, if you want it that badly, I'll trade for your truck and the $3,000."

"Yeah, thought you would, you swindler."

Both men, he would later tell, laughed as they shook hands and exchanged keys and paperwork to their respective vehicles. Now *The Weasel* was ready to return to the United States. He had a nondescript vehicle that would not draw attention, forged paperwork that would pass ordinary inspection and a lot of cash still left from the bank heist. He crossed the border into the states without even receiving a second glance. While in Mexico, he had let his hair and beard grow. He also had eaten well and gained a considerable amount of weight. This transition resulted in a complete makeover. However, the one thing he could not change was his height. He was barely five feet tall and if it weren't for his hardened features and beard might have been mistaken for a seventh or eighth grader. He tried wearing boots with a higher heel to appear taller but found they just hurt his feet and made him clumsy.

It was Thanksgiving when *The Weasel* finally made his way back to Jefferson City. He drove into town and took a room at a cheap motel. Much to his delight, no one recognized him. This, of course, bolstered his confidence. It was getting late and *The Weasel* was hungry. He asked the desk clerk if there were any restaurants still serving since it was a holiday. The clerk told him the truck stop at the edge of town was open 24/7 and was probably still serving. It is told *The Weasel* then drove to the truck stop where he indulged himself in a delightful turkey dinner, with all the traditional trimmings. The meal even came with a generous slice of pumpkin pie topped with a dollop of whipped cream, he would later quip.

Present at the truck stop were several uniformed law enforcement officers on their "lunch" break also having Thanksgiving dinner but not even one glanced in his direction. *The Weasel* said he surmised his physical transformation and long absence masked his true identity so much so that not even the law enforcement community recognized him. He had also been dressing more stylish, he said, thanks to the bank money, and changing his mannerisms so as to perpetrate the ideal deception. So far, his disguise proved effective. Even the recent tattooing which he freely exhibited, added to the deception.

The Weasel walked to the register to pay for his meal and took a copy of the local newspaper with him as he left. Although he didn't need to generate any income, at least not for the time being nor even for the foreseeable future, he wanted to take a job so he could continue to use his cover to scope out easy marks and not become stagnant. With what was left of the bank loot, he planned to buy a small farm on the outskirts of Jefferson City "if the price was right."

The first job opportunity that caught his eye was an advertisement for a "Mall Santa."

"Well, well. How appropriate," *The Weasel* thought. Because he had let his hair and his beard grow out, he looked more like a jolly elf than a bank robber. Additionally, all of his hair had turned white due to all the stress he had experienced in the recent past, giving him an actual authentic "Santa" look. He took this as an omen. And the Friday after Thanksgiving, he proceeded to the employment office at the mall and submitted his application. With his fraudulent credentials in hand, he waited patiently in the lobby for his interview.

"What have we here?" Wilson Cranston, the supervisor conducting the interviews, asked and smiling, said, "You look more like Santa than Santa. Don't tell me your first name is Chris as in *Chris Kringle?*" Without giving *The Weasel* time to reply, Cranston added with a broad smile, "If your background checks out, you got the job."

The Weasel squirmed at the thought of a background check. Although *The Weasel* used the name of a deceased acquaintance from a different state on the fake IDs, he was not sure how things would pan out. He said to Cranston, "I should tell you that I left my last job under duress. My boss had a conflict with me and more-or-less forced me to leave. I don't think he will give me a very good recommendation. If this is a problem, I'll look elsewhere for employment although I'm not confident anyone would hire me without a recommendation."

Cranston, being a compassionate man and obviously somewhat naive, apparently nodded his head and said, "I was in a similar situation once myself. In fact, despite a bad recommendation, I was hired to fill the position I now hold so I understand your predicament. Tell you what, I'm willing to take a chance on you. Hopefully, it will not backfire. I'll give you the job since it is seasonal. If things work out for both of us, I may be able to give you something more permanent. What do you say?"

"ABSOLUTELY! Thank you so much for trusting in me and giving me a chance. I promise you will not be disappointed."

Cranston, it is said, told *The Weasel* to fill out the forms and report first thing the following Monday morning in order to get outfitted and trained in his Santa duties. They shook hands and parted. *The Weasel* said he whistled Jingle Bells all the way to his truck smug in the success of what he considered to be the perfect con. He admitted later he felt he was now in a position to scope easy targets to burglarize in the mall and didn't even have to sneak around to do so. He said he could be brazen without creating suspicion. Also, he apparently reasoned, the spare cash would allow him to accumulate funds so as not only to help acquire the coveted farm property he had always dreamed of but maintain and improve it as well.

LIFE HAD PRETTY MUCH returned to normal for the *R*U*1*2s*. The families who lived on Melrose Lane and in the surrounding communities certainly had even more reason to be thankful this Thanksgiving. At church services and other community gatherings, prayers were rendered thanking God for my safe return and for all the other blessings that were being bestowed upon us and our community with each passing day.

Rhymin' Sally, as was expected, was an extremely enthusiastic student and the most popular kindergartener. Her classmates swarmed around her during the recesses because they loved to listen to her talk. One day during class, Ms. Hollenbeck, the kindergarten teacher, asked the children to each take turns telling the class what they wanted to be when they grew up. When Sally's turn came, she boldly stood and stated:

> *When I grow up I want to be just like Shacoo, that's who!*
> *She always knows just what to do. She's so brave, kind and true.*
> *There's no one known to me or you, that's quite like Shacoo.*

Well, needless to say, Ms. Hollenbeck had also fallen under Sally's spell, much like the rest of us, and it is said, smiled to herself thinking: *She is not at all meek and mild. I will have to explore ways to express my thoughts unbridled. Sally, truly, is a gifted child.*

CHAPTER FIVE

POLAR EYES

The Christmas break was fast approaching, and all of us, the *R*U*1*2s*, that is, were getting eager for the two-week reprieve from school. The weather had cooperated and Jefferson City was blanketed in a coat of sparkling fresh white snow. Soon, almost every yard had a snowman standing sentinel. We began challenging one another to see who could be the most creative in adorning our respective snowmen. During a meeting at the clubhouse, the *R*U*1*2s*, as a group, decided to conduct a snow sculpturing contest and select a weekly favorite. We decided on no prizes; only the honor of having the best snowman that particular week. We posted the names of the weekly winners and a photograph of their sculptures on the bulletin board inside the clubhouse. Some of the R*U*1*2s, who entered the contest and some who didn't, I mention below.

Carly and Tanner Atkinson built two snowmen, one representing Darth Vader and the other Luke Skywalker dueling with the boys' Star Wars swords.

Scooter, Sonny and Toby, with Rhymin' Sally's help, decided to recreate in their snow sculpture the three little kittens who had lost their mittens—which turned out better by far than any of them expected. Also, to Sally's delight, kittens and mittens rhymed. Sonny's mother provided them with food coloring to tint the snow and make the colorful mittens. Being inspired, the four located some old sweaters in the lost and found at school that were to be thrown out and dressed the kittens "in sweaters that matched their mittens," at least according to Rhymin' Sally.

Mohawk, so named for his haircut, dressed his snowman like an Indian chief, and created a life-size sculpture that caused passersby to look twice to confirm it was not real. Mo had an Indian headdress stored in his closet from a former Halloween costume which he donated to his snowman who he dubbed *Chief White Horse* thus giving credentials to his first work of art.

Pineapple, our club member from Hawaii, formed from the soft snow a Hawaiian queen which rivaled Mohawk's chief. Like Mohawk's sculpture, Pineapple's was also life-size and generated a debate as to whose snowman or snow woman was the best. Pineapple's queen, however, wore authentic traditional Hawaiian garb consisting of a grass skirt and a Hawaiian lei which made his sculpture the most realistic.

Dusty and Rusty, the identical twins, chose to build a dog house with a representation of their dog, Maya, peeking from within. When it was complete, the twins took Maya out to show her the look-alike. Excitedly, she scurried around in the fluffy white snow, and if it wasn't for her movement and black eyes, she would have blended in with her surroundings and perhaps have been lost until the spring thaw.

Cupcake, our fussy ten-year old, and scourge, chose not to participate and instead boycotted the displays claiming they were defiling the snow and mocking Mother Nature.

Penny and Kitty Montgomery created a snowman sitting in a kitty car in honor of their father's business, Montgomery Auto Sales. We suspected their parents had provided assistance judging from its realistic appearance.

Willy and Wiki Sanders, our brother and sister team, could not agree on a theme so they just went with the traditional snowman. As it would turn out, it was so bland they did not merit even an honorable mention.

Tank, Genius and I conspired to create a replica of *The Cat*. *The Cat* was a burglar who had terrorized our neighborhood in the recent past but was captured with the help of the *R*U*1*2s* and sentenced to a long term of imprisonment. Our cat was a big snow ball with a smaller head and four paws sticking out and our cat was poised in a striking position. Between the three of us, we came up with a black ski mask, a black cape and a black satchel which had been used by *The Cat,* the real one and not our copycat, to carry burglary tools. This satchel, however, was ultimately encased in snow. We cut and inserted cardboard ears representing cat ears into the ski mask and also cut cat paws from cardboard, painted them black and inserted three popsicle stick sized claws into each of the four paws. Looking at our finished product, I shivered—and it wasn't just from the cold.

Although the infamous gang known as Gang Green was not part of the R*U*1*2 neighborhood, the Greens, as they were often referred to, were our cross-town rivals. They asked if they could join in the "Snowman Challenge." We unanimously agreed, that is with Cupcake dissenting, to let them in on the fun. The Greens had been very helpful in the capture of *The Cat* and consequently had formed a bond of sorts with the *R*U*1*2s*. According to Rhymin' Sally,

> *The Greens act rough and tough*
> *and hard to bluff.*
> *In reality, they're pretty cool*
> *And always quick to duel.*
> *They have strange talk*
> *And they swagger when they walk.*

Genius lived in a big house on a big lot and the front yard was extensive. He offered half of his snow and half of his yard to the Greens to use to erect their snowman since the Greens lived on the other side of town and the *R*U*1*2s* were not allowed to stray that far from home and thus would have been unavailable to view the Greens' entry and render a vote. Bonz, the leader of the Greens, Slick, the second in command and Spyder, who had recently been commissioned a lieutenant, readily accepted the offer. The race was on and the competition, as expected, would be intense.

"Hey, Man, cool. Can we get started right away or do you need more of a head start?" I remember Bonz asking in his usual sarcastic quip.

"We're really anxious to see what you three racketeers come up with." Genius muttered rolling his eyes at Tank and me. Fortunately, the Greens thought Genius had referred to them as the three "musketeers." Otherwise, Genius would have come away looking like a raccoon sporting two traditional black eyes and maybe even a broken nose.

"Yeah, if you're throwing down the gauntlet, sissy, consider the challenge met. Our snowman will make yours appear to be what it truly will be—a pitiful and ineffective attempt by a group of amateurs to look like something it isn't."

"Yep! Says you!" Genius replied never resisting an opportunity to taunt the Greens even though he really had grown to like them. We had a lot of fun bantering back and forth with the Greens. We just hoped the Greens had a sense of humor and would not be sore losers. The Greens had other ideas and a different slant on the outcome.

And so, the competition commenced in earnest. It was obvious that the Greens were up to the task. It was so intense that Genius was beginning to wonder if there would be enough snow on the Greens' side of the lawn to finish the monster project they started. The Greens snowman began taking shape and soon was of gigantic proportions. It was every bit as tall as the first story of Genius' house and maybe even taller. It was sculptured into a polar bear. Somehow the Greens managed to insert two battery operated flashlights containing green bulbs to serve as eye sockets. This created an eerie appearance which easily frightened the petrified, paranoid and those with shatter-pated imaginations. It served as a magnet, however, for the curious, fanatical and eccentric.

"Yeah, too bad we can't hook up a speaker system and play scary sounds," Bonz said in a taunting cadence.

"You turkeys," Genius countered, "it's not Halloween; it's Christmas. I know how you love the ghoulish aura that surrounds Halloween, but, since your 'thing' is in my yard, I would ask that you hold back just a bit in honor of the Christmas holiday. Come to think of it, would you consider one red eye and one green eye?"

"Hey, man, that would be cool but we don't have any red lights on the stuff we use. Everything we use comes in green, like us. Besides, that's our trademark." With that all of the Greens laughed so boisterously that it brought old Mrs. Broilington out onto the neighboring porch to see what all the commotion was about." Not bad for a woman with a severe hearing disorder, or so we all thought. As she herself had admitted, "I am deaf in one ear and can't hear out of the other."

As Bonz, Slick and Spyder ambled off down the street, Genius yelled after them, "Stop by the clubhouse tomorrow after lunch. Everyone should have had a chance to see the new entry by then. We'll be voting on the overall 'Best in the Show' and you'll have the opportunity to congratulate the winner and you know who that will be."

"Yeah, we'll be there to accept the first place prize and offer the *R*U*1*2s* our condolences," Bonz retorted.

"Fat chance. Anyway, there are no prizes, only the honor of winning and having your name inscribed on the bulletin board at the clubhouse until school starts after Christmas break."

"No way, man. It sounds like withdrawing the prize is tantamount to a concession. We can see why you might throw in the towel. But, withholding the prize is like dangling a carrot and then throwing it away. Taint fair!"

"Okay, tell you what we'll do. If you win, we'll buy each of you a onetime pass to Glacier Ice Rink."

"Well, now, that's different. Anything for a free skate from a cheapskate. Good luck on coming in second. You don't have a chance to take first. If, however, by some strange quirk and universes collide and you do win first prize," Bonz shot back, "We'll buy *you* a one week pass to the new Glacier Ice Rink. No, make that a season pass."

"Wow! You have plans to rob a bank or maybe come into an unexpected inheritance?"

"Yeah, well let's just say we don't expect to lose. To lose to losers would be like a gazelle being outrun by a snail."

"Then you better get used to eating crow because that might be your only diet for the next few months," Genius snapped back.

PENNY AND KITTY'S PARENTS wanted to recognize the exploits of the *R*U*1*2s*, so their father, Greg Montgomery called the newspaper. Cardel West, having just graduated from journalism school, was assigned the least important stories so he was given the pink message slip by his editor which instructed him to call Mr. Montgomery back to see what all the fuss was about.

West called Mr. Montgomery immediately as things were pretty slow in the newspaper office that week. Mr. Montgomery explained to West what the *R*U*1*2s* were doing and West apparently was thoroughly captivated by the story. Being low man on the totem pole, West also did his own photography. So with camera, pad and pen in hand, he went to the Melrose neighborhood and sought out the Montgomery residence.

Penny and Kitty's parents invited West in, and after a brief conversation, took him for a tour of the neighborhood pointing out the various snow sculptures and the names of the individuals who created them. West took pictures of each and every sculpture and noted on his pad the names of those who had fashioned them. He was informed that the *R*U*1*2s* planned to meet the following afternoon to select the overall "Best in the Show." West assured them he would be in attendance when the voting took place.

When the R*U*1*2s met the next day, the selection was unanimous. The *Jefferson City Times'* editor was so moved by the story when it was presented to him by West that he elected to give West a blurb on the top half of the front page. When the evening paper hit the streets, the following headline story appeared:

POLAR EYES TAKES FIRST PRIZE

Polar Eyes, as seen in the photograph below, took the "Best in the Show" in a neighborhood snow sculpturing contest. The contest was sponsored by a club of children known as the *R*U*1*2s*. Each week, for six consecutive weeks, a new winner was selected (photographs of the entries and winners are pictured on page E-4) and the winners posted on a bulletin board in the *R*U*1*2s'* clubhouse situated in the middle of the Pearson Apple Orchard on Melrose Avenue.

At the end of the contest, the *R*U*1*2s* selected from the six winners, the "Best in the Show." Polar Eyes, it so happened, was the entry of a rival group of teens known as the Gang Greens. The Gang Greens had been invited by the *R*U*1*2s* to participate in the contest, and both groups competed in the spirit of Christmas and the Gang Greens ended up garnering the coveted prize. Polar Eyes, a giant polar bear with flashing green eyes, was the clear winner. The children did not have actual physical prizes to award. However, the honor of winning was having the winner's name posted on the *R*U*1*2s* Board of Honor.

The Jefferson City Times, in a show of support and goodwill, will be awarding a $100 cash prize to the winner and has agreed to sponsor the second and perhaps succeeding winter contests. We feel that the two groups, even though they are rivals, were able to join together in this worthwhile winter event which was included in the community's Tour of Lights. We proudly commend all those who entered and participated in this event. Good job, *R*U*1*2s* and congratulations Gang Greens. Keep up the good work. The community anxiously awaits next year's entries.

The *R*U*1*2s* and especially the Gang Greens were very excited about the headlines and front page story and by having their snowmen featured in the newspaper. Both groups felt it would help in their respective recruitment programs as well as the future relationship between the two groups. They proved competition was not a bad thing.

"So, what are you chumps, I mean champs, going to do with your prize money?" Genius sarcastically asked as he taunted Bonz.

"Hey, Man, we won fair-and-square. Don't be a spoil sport." Bonz responded, "We were thinkin' among ourselves that maybe we could split the prize money since the *R*U*1*2s* sponsored this gig. We think that is the only fair thing to do. Or, in the alternative, it could be used to buy Christmas gifts for the less fortunate. But, Man, remember you still owe us skate passes—no reneging on a bet." Bonz, then raising both eyebrows, shook a threatening finger in Genius' direction.

Genius saw merit in Bonz' offer to buy gifts and distribute them to the less fortunate. He then offered the services of the

R*U*1*2s in the purchase and distribution of the gifts. He said that the share the *R*U*1*2s* would receive, should the Gang Greens chose not to exercise that option, would be to use the funds to benefit the less fortunate anyway. "We intend to honor our commitment and have no intention whatsoever to renege on our bet. The Greens won fair and square." With that, Genius retrieved from a folded white paper envelope he had in his jacket pocket a dozen daily passes to Glacier Ice Rink and passed them out to the Greens, and as he did so, shook each of their hands.

It was agreed that the *R*U*1*2s* and the Greens would make the Christmas event an annual affair and a charitable fund raiser. They also agreed to expand the joint venture between the two groups during future Thanksgiving holidays. Everyone agreed that both would be noble endeavors and of benefit to the community and especially to the have nots.

"What a difference an award makes," Rhymin' Sally said following the departure of the Gang Greens.

> *In the not too distant past, a dark cloud the Gang Greens did cast.*
> *We learned to run instead of having fun.*
> *Now all that is reversed and it's not something we rehearsed.*
> *All's well that ends well—a story we can forever tell.*

"Well said dear Sal, but only time will tell," Genius said kicking himself for yielding to Rhymin' Sally's spell. Even at my age, I, too, often find myself engaging in the *R*U*1*2s* rhyming rage which I'm sure to the reader will be compelling.

CHAPTER SIX
MALL SANTA

The Weasel was excited about starting his new job as Santa. He arrived early for his appointment to be fitted with his tailored Santa suit. The wardrobe custodian remarked that *The Weasel's* white hair and beard were in character, and therefore, it was unnecessary to fit him with a white wig and beard. This pleased *The Weasel* because he didn't relish the idea of wearing either one, especially any scratchy ones. After being outfitted and groomed, he was escorted back to Wilson Cranston's office for Cranston's final stamp of approval. Wilson was pleased at how splendid *The Weasel* looked. He would be the "quintessential Santa," he told *The Weasel*. After Cranston went over a script with *The Weasel*, he took *The Weasel* to the center of the mall where the North Pole was replicated and ushered him to the big red velvet chair situated in the center of the mall's Christmas display. There the notorious fugitive from justice, now a Christmas icon and the center of attention, would be hidden in plain view.

There was a brightly colored train that carried children in a circle around the replicated North Pole taking them past artificial shop fronts sporting every kind of delight a child could want: toy shops, candy stores, pet shops and variety stores loaded with stuffed animals of every description, movie theaters, arcades and sporting goods stores. At the end of the ride, the children were invited to visit Santa and share with him, as they sat on his lap, what they wanted for Christmas. Having their appetites whetted by the train ride, none of the children had difficulty in making their requests known. None needed to be coaxed. Their quandary was in prioritizing their gifts as Santa, overwhelmed by the demands, was required to impose a quota system so that no child would be without a gift.

The Weasel soon grew weary of having children climb all over him and listening to them drone on and on about what they wanted for Christmas. He knew, however, that he must play the part in order to pursue his scheme to scope out the stores in the mall in an effort to determine how to best breach their respective security systems. The unwary shop owners were delighted with Santa's visits and his spread of holiday cheer. Little did they know or even suspect he was "casing the joint."

Each morning and each afternoon on his break, *The Weasel* would walk the length of the mall visiting the various retail outlets. His disguise could not have been any more effective. He mentally made note of which businesses would be the easiest to burglarize. He did not keep written lists because he did not want anything tangible to link him to any crimes he was contemplating committing. He was becoming more brazen with the passage of each day and smug in his belief that he could operate without detection for as long as he desired. Nothing or no one could stand in his way. He was destined to reign undetected the rest of his days as the undisputed "King Con."

One afternoon, as *The Weasel* was strolling through the mall dressed as Santa, he was spotted by Genius, Tank and me as we were shopping for Christmas gifts. As we casually meandered along the corridors, I suddenly stopped frozen in my tracks. The man dressed as Santa was not Santa, it was *The Weasel!* The boys had advanced a few steps beyond apparently before becoming aware that I was no longer at their side. Turning around, Genius later said they noticed the bewildered expression on my face. Concerned, he asked, "Shacoo, are you all right? What's wrong?"

"That's him." I whispered frantically, pointing in *The Weasel's* direction.

"That's who?" Tank asked and squinted.

"That…that's the man who kidnapped me," I said. "Even though he is disguised as Santa, his eyes and his size say otherwise."

"You're beginning to sound like Rhymin' Sally," Tank said. Later he apologized and said he should have appreciated the serious nature of the encounter.

"What about his eyes and his size?" Genius asked.

"I'd know those eyes anywhere and there are not too many grown men that short. Having stared into those evil eyes during my captivity, they are forever etched in my mind. There's no doubt. Those are the eyes of my abductor. 'Santa' to you but *The Weasel* to me. I'd bet my life on it."

I watched as Tank and Genius turned and stared at the re-
treating figure as he disappeared into Café Court. It was obvious
The Weasel, alias Santa, was oblivious to our presence. Bundled in
our winter garb, we were, no doubt, unrecognizable. *The Weasel*
seemed preoccupied by the task at hand—preparing for his first
big hit as a Santa.

"Come on, let's follow him," Tank suggested.

"Not me." I said defiantly. "I don't want to be anywhere near
him; not now or ever again."

"Genius, you take Shacoo home before she is spotted," Tank
said. "I'll bird-dog Santa for the next hour or two and call you
later on my cell phone. Be sure to stay close to yours."

"You sure you want to do that?" I asked in a shaky voice. "He
is very dangerous you know. He threatened me more than once.
Not only is he dangerous, he is also desperate."

"Yeah, Tank. You know what desperate people are capable
of. You had an encounter with one just barely a year ago. Don't
tell me you've already forgotten *The Cat,*" Genius reminded.

"Oh, no. I'll never forget *The Cat.* I just don't want this weasel
to harm any more innocent people. For what he did to Shacoo,
he deserves at a minimum, ten life sentences."

"Looks like we have a pattern developing here: *The Cat* and
now *The Weasel,*" Genius said. "Let's just hope we don't end up
with a zoo full of villains."

I didn't, at that time, find Genius' comment particularly
amusing. Incensed, I blurted, "Oh, very funny. This is not comical in the least. Wipe the smiles from your faces."

The discussion did ease the situation somewhat and it was
obvious that I had withstood the initial shock and was now more
at ease. I learned to be brave under stress and now was more determined than ever to expose *The Weasel's* cover. Fear had turned into
dread; dread into determination; and determination into a call for

retribution. *The Weasel's* fate now rested squarely on my shoulders and those of my two companions, Tank and Genius.

"Shacoo, we're sorry," Genius said. "We didn't mean to make light of the matter. It's a coping mechanism, I guess. Come on, I'll walk you home." And turning to Tank, Genius said, "Tank, remember I have my cell phone, if you need help call. But, by all means, take no chances. We don't need someone else to worry about."

"Will do." Tank replied. "You two go on. I don't want *The Weasel* to get too far ahead of me." And with that, Tank headed in the direction of Café Court.

As Tank entered Café Court, he said he spotted *The Weasel,* alias Santa, standing in line at the pizza counter. He said he then immediately turned and faced in the other direction to avoid detection by the pretend Santa. Tank said he was concerned that if he was recognized that would spook the villain off before we had a chance to ID him and have him arrested. Tank said he got in a long line at the TCBY counter and shuffled along sneaking peeks at *The Weasel,* alias Santa, as he moved up. He said he watched *The Weasel* pay for his pizza and a soda with a large bill and no doubt, because of the crowded tables in Café Court, moved on out into the mall. Tank, said *The Weasel* then found an empty bench and sat down looking in all directions making sure, obviously, that he was not being tailed. "I would be paranoid, too, if I was him," Tank would later say. "He certainly looked suspicious the way he was constantly looking over his shoulder. It was as though he was expecting something or someone to jump out of the shadows and nab him."

When *The Weasel* finished his lunch, Tank said, *The Weasel* got up and discarded his trash in a receptacle and ambled on as if he was satisfied he was not being tailed. Tank followed he said, "in hot pursuit." *The Weasel* strolled slowly past selected stores and probed each very intently. *The Weasel,* according to Tank, actually entered one of the high-end jewelry stores, and walked around looking in the display cases as if he were taking mental snapshots of the various items of jewelry. Tank said he surmised *The Weasel* was "casing the joint" as those in *The Weasel's* trade would likely say.

After *The Weasel* had made his way out of the jewelry store, Tank said he followed *The Weasel* back to his Santa station. Tank said there was a long line of children waiting for "Santa's" return. *The Weasel,* still not fond of having children climb all over him, we surmised, tolerated them for the good of the order—his order. Fortunately, he had not spotted Genius, Tank or me. As for Tank, Tank was also becoming adept at avoiding detection, and as we would learn later, *The Weasel* had no clue he was being followed.

With *The* Weasel back at work, Tank decided it was safe for him to leave and hook up with Genius and me. When the three of us congregated, Tank briefed us on *The Weasel's* actions and what he suspected *The Weasel* was up to. We then began hatching a plan. First of all, we agreed we would have to hide inside the mall so that when it closed we could continue to watch every move of the would-be thief. Tank offered to be the one to be on watch the first evening but Genius told him it was too dangerous for him to do it alone. Tank and Genius agreed to team up to watch and wait. I was made privy to the plan so that if anything went wrong, I would know and be able to summon help should the need arise. We would all make sure our cell phones were charged and working before we undertook such a dangerous mission. We all agreed there was no room for any slip-ups and all risks needed to be calculated ones. None of us could later explain the premonition we had that that night would be the night *The*

Weasel would strike and the night his criminal spree would come to a screeching end.

TANK AND GENIUS HEADED back to the mall to scope out possible hiding places. They were in luck. The trash was collected before the mall closed for the night and new plastic liners were being inserted. Tank and Genius decided they would split up and each would hide in a trash receptacle to avoid detection. They were afraid if they hid in one of the department stores dressing rooms, they would be detected, or at the very least, set off the store's alarm upon moving about and certainly upon exiting.

A light snow was falling as the mall began to empty and shoppers headed home. Tank and Genius would later tell me they languished on a bench waiting for the coast to clear. Soon as everyone had left the area they had scoped out, and taking advantage of the opportunity, slipped into separate trash receptacles and hunkered down for the long haul. Genius later said he realized that this was probably not a great idea since they would have the security patrol to contend with, and with their visibility being impaired by the sides of the receptacles, would be unable to determine with any real accuracy whether the coast was or was not clear. He said he just hoped when he and Tank lifted the lids to peer out, they wouldn't be detected by either *The Weasel* or the security patrol. Tank and Genius both said later, they realized that the odds were really stacked against them.

Fortunately, Tank and Genius were not be missed by their parents as they apparently had convinced their parents they would be spending the night camped in the woods practicing winter survival skills with their Boy Scout troop. This was, in fact, what they originally had planned to do until we had spotted

The Weasel that afternoon at the mall. If their surveillance failed, they knew their parents would be unforgiving and the consequences would be severe. There was little doubt that their plan had to succeed. And if their hunch was correct, my abductor, the great imposter and the would-be burglar, would be caught at his own game and be behind bars before daybreak.

As soon as they heard the security guard's Segway pass, they climbed out of their hiding places and went into the area of Café Court where they could watch the jewelry store from a more inconspicuous and more advantageous position. They crouched down for what, they said, seemed like an eternity and then their vigilance was finally rewarded. *The Weasel*, still in his Santa attire, hastened along the corridor looking in every direction. They watched as he took out a packet of lock picks and started working on the gate that secured the jewelry store where he earlier had been observed. Much to their amazement, *The Weasel* had the lock picked in a matter of seconds. They said they looked at each other in wonder. "How'd he do that?" Tank supposedly asked Genius. What the boys didn't know was that *The Weasel* for the past week had very carefully surveyed the alarm system in the jewelry store. He deliberately managed to be in a strategic position in order to watch the very young, inexperienced night clerk punch in the code that would arm or more importantly disarm the system. The clerk apparently took no particular note of anyone watching as she entered the four digit code numbers while simultaneously chewing gum and chatting with her boyfriend on her cell phone.

The Weasel was in, having disarmed the alarm, and began unlocking the display counters with his set of magic keys. Once all the counters were unlocked he retrieved a black velvet pouch from his pocket, and opening it, very carefully began to fill it with the precious items that were displayed before him. His eyes beamed like stars as he gathered in the precious gem stones, Tank and Genius would later report.

Tank said he nudged Genius as they observed *The Weasel's* stealth. He said they were transfixed by the efficiency and nimbleness of someone who had great skill and experience in the practice of his craft, albeit one that was not thought to be tolerated in a civilized society. Soon Tank had his cell phone pressed to his ear. "Dad, it's Tank.... yes, I know Dad, it's late but.... Dad, please listen to me! Okay, but first I want you to be aware that Genius and I did not go camping as planned but instead hid out in the mall to watch a man we suspected of having kidnapped Shacoo. Dad... I know and will explain later. No... I can't now. Yes, we're sure it's him. Shacoo even identified him—sort of. He was in a Santa suit and with the beard it was hard to tell, but that isn't why I'm calling. Genius and I just watched him break into Corrigon-Bradington Jewelers and he is now in the process of stealing everything in sight."

"Tank, you stay where you are and out of sight. Where are you exactly?" came his father's voice.

"We are in the front of Café Court hiding behind the counter at the courtesy counter. We can see everything that is happening at CBJ."

"Okay, but stay hidden and don't do anything that will put either of you in harm's way. I'll send a squad car and be there as quickly as I can. Under no circumstances are you or Genius to break cover or try to be heroes! Do I make myself clear?"

"Okay, Dad, but what do we do if he tries to leave. My impression is he is going to split forever once he cleans out the jewelry store. Whoa! I just saw him stuff the Santa suit into a trash container and he looks like he's ready to bolt. Should we follow him?"

"NO! That would be too dangerous. It was only by luck that Shacoo escaped. If indeed he is the kidnapper he will not think twice of injuring or holding you two boys hostage. Do not put yourselves in danger under any circumstances! This is a job for trained police personnel and even for them it would be risky. Do I make myself clear?"

"That's affirmative."

"By the way, stay on the line and do not hang up. And be sure to turn down the volume on your cell. Do you read?"

"That's another affirmative."

"I've just radioed the patrol unit in the area," Tank's father announced. "They will meet me there. I'm now in my car and in transit and will be there in just a few minutes."

Tank said he could hear the roar of the engine over the phone just as Genius elbowed him and pointed in the direction of the jewelry store.

"Dad. Dad, he's left our immediate area. We could follow to see what exit he is planning to use. That would give you an edge when you get here."

"Tank! You are NOT, I repeat, NOT to pursue. I'm almost there. Stay where you are! Go ahead and hang up and do not hesitate to call me on your cell phone if you need me. I will keep my cell phone close by as well as my police radio."

Tank and Genius later told me the urge to follow was overwhelming. They had a way out. Tank's Dad hadn't actually said Genius was not to pursue—only Tank! Tank said he looked at Genius, who was standing there nervously waiting. It was imperative that someone tail the pretend Santa turned burglar. Otherwise, *The Weasel* would be like a needle in a haystack—impossible to find.

"Genius, you have to follow him," Tank supposedly said. "I have strict orders not to. Dad implied you were not to pursue but didn't say that directly. You follow and I'll circle around to the other side and try to meet you there."

"Works for me. Stay close to your cell phone and I'll do the same. That way we can keep track of each other. I'd better get going before he completely disappears."

Genius, he said, then left to take up the pursuit. Tank said he then circled Café Court and came out on the other side. He did not see *The Weasel* at first but upon closer inspection saw him slinking against the walls trying to look inconspicuous. Tank reported *The Weasel's* location to Genius. "It looks like *The Weasel* is headed for the west exit," he said. Tank said he then punched the number of his father's cell phone.

"Dad, it's Tank. Go to the west exit. I repeat, the west exit."

Tank's father said later he was perturbed by the fact that Tank had disobeyed his explicit instructions but he was also proud that his son had the initiative and courage to follow through on a matter of such great importance.

Tank's father took over from there, as we would later learn. He directed his unit to the west exit where they spotted *The Weasel* who had just cleared the doors and was sprinting towards his truck. Some of the loot fell to the pavement as he ran. The police swarmed around *The Weasel* before he could unlock his truck and soon had him contained. Tank and Genius, it turned out, were not far behind and said they watched the whole event as it unfolded. They apparently high-fived each other and then waited for the fallout. Tank later said he knew he was going to be in big trouble but felt it was worth it all in light of the result. Throughout the whole takedown, Tank and Genius said they had remained "cool, calm and collected." When it was over, they said, they were a little jittery and somewhat apprehensive. Tank's father would later say it was more like "nervous expectation."

The Weasel was squirming around on the pavement trying to free himself from the handcuffs as two officers held him down while a third searched him. *The Weasel*, Tank's father would later say, was reluctant to relinquish what was left of his recently acquired booty and was very vocal about what he perceived as rough treatment from the police. As Tank's father approached Tank and Genius, Tank apparently shrunk from his father's gaze. He said he knew he was in trouble and wasn't sure he could talk his way out of the dilemma.

"You boys show me where the burglary took place," Tank's father instructed. This was not the time or place to scold his son, he later would be heard to say. He said he knew, that but for the gallant efforts of Genius and his son, *The Weasel's* plot would not have been foiled.

Tank and Genius led Tank's father to the location of Corrigon-Bradington Jewelers. The crime scene investigation unit followed and when they arrived at the jewelry store, the team took over the investigation gathering evidence and dusting for prints. Tank's father called the owner of the store at the telephone number listed on the "In Case of Emergency" notification placard on the window adjacent to the folding metal gate at the front of the store.

Tank's father said he knew that processing the crime scene would take the better part of the night so he released Tank and Genius to one of the detectives with instructions to return the boys to their respective residences. In doing so, he apparently said to Tank and Genius: "You deliberately disobeyed my explicit instructions. Catching a bad guy does not warrant putting yourselves or others at risk. I'm just glad you're both safe and sound and no one has been injured. We'll talk more about this later. For now, suffice it to say I'm proud of both of you for the bravery you displayed during this whole perilous event. Not only did the two of you prevent a heist, but you also were instrumental in catching a notorious thief, someone who has been a blight on this community. And as you both already suspect, we have determined that the culprit was also Shacoo's abductor. But for your efforts, he may never have been captured." Tank's father, it is told, then put his arms around both boys' shoulders and introduced them to his partner as "genuine heroes." They were then whisked away from the scene.

"Wow, I thought we were facing the death penalty," Tank reputedly whispered to Genius as the two followed the detective to the parking lot.

"We are not out of the woods yet," Genius predictably responded. "So, don't get your hopes up. We may still be facing the firing squad or something just as bad." Tank apparently just hung his head and shook it from side-to-side. Sensing the need to be positive, Genius said he added, "Look at it this way. We helped crack the case and made your father look good. What's so bad about that? We should be commended and not condemned. I think our parents will agree with that assessment and our punishment will be minimal…if at all."

Tank said he smiled at Genius. In the final analysis, they both agreed they had done the right thing. They wouldn't have done anything different, both later told me. They apparently were exhausted from the long day and the excitement and were glad to be heading home. Genius said he suddenly realized he had not reported in to his parents and could still be in hot water when he returned home. He said it was his turn to hang his head. "Oh, geeze," he reputedly had said as he gritted his teeth and cringed at the thought of what might be in store for him when he came face-to-face with his parents. He surmised it would not be a very pretty scene. For the moment, he said he just took a deep breath and hoped his parents would be understanding.

Tank, on the other hand, I later learned, was becoming more optimistic in light of Genius's proclamation and his father's acclamation. He felt his father was a reasonable man, and being a champion of justice, would rally behind him and carefully weigh the pros and cons of forgiving his disobedience and deception. Only after he did so, would his father render a decision. And only if it was warranted, would he give his unconditional pardon. After all, Tank's father would later say, "How can I fault my son if, when faced with the same dilemma, I would have made the same choices." It was also learned that Genius' father, after the same careful reflection, arrived at the same conclusion. Tank and Genius would later say, "All's well that ends well. Just so much water under the bridge. The past is history; the future still a mystery!"

THE WEASEL WAS PLACED under arrest, read his rights and transported to the county detention facility. He was first placed in an interrogation room, and when police officers tried to question him, we were told, he became confrontational and demanded the presence of an attorney. Upon having invoked his right to remain silent and be afforded the right to confer with an attorney, the officers, of course, ceased questioning him. *The Weasel* was then fingerprinted and photographed. His personal items were collected and placed in a bag marked with his identifying information and he was transported to the county jail. I can rather imagine he was not his usual arrogant and obnoxious self—no longer the "cat's meow" as he had always bragged.

Early the following morning, *The Weasel* was brought before the presiding judge, The Honorable Rosco Q. Sheriden, a gruff but fair judge nearing retirement age, advised *The* Weasel of his rights and the nature of the charges he was facing. Because I had been liberated alive and unharmed, that made the kidnapping a bailable offense. However, because of *The Weasel's* pattern of criminality, bond was set at an even $1,000,000. *The Weasel* would have been unable to post the bond even if the proceeds from the bank heist had not been confiscated. At least for now, *The Weasel* would be removed from society and would languish in the county detention center to ponder his own fate.

THE SAME DAY *THE Weasel* appeared in court, police officers contacted my parents and requested that they bring me to the detention facility to view a lineup. They readily agreed but when they told me, I was hesitant to go. After some coaxing, I decided I should go because if this "Santa" was indeed *the* kidnapper, other children could be in danger and I didn't want what happened to me to happen to them. My father was likewise distressed but for another reason. He had violated his own personal code and the law by falsifying the DNA results. If I identified my kidnapper, as he assumed I would, he would have no recourse but to confess to what he had done and suffer the consequences of his actions. So, putting our private anxieties aside, we left for the detention facility not knowing what to expect but knowing we had to do the right thing.

When we arrived at the detention facility, we were met by Tank's father who escorted us to the location where the lineup was to be held. Tank's father, apparently noticing that I was nervous, put a calming hand on my shoulder and said we could do a photographic lineup rather than a live one. A photo lineup consisted of a grouping of mug shots of the suspected perpetrator together with various individuals similar in looks and size to that of the suspected perpetrator. The witness would then attempt to identify a suspect without having to view him or her in person. I weighed the choices and knew sooner or later that I would have to come face-to-face with my abductor and to prolong the agony would only intensify my anxiety. However, my anxiety was erased when I was told I could view the lineup from behind a two-way mirror.

In the criminal justice system, I was told, a live viewing was thought to be the most reliable and thus preferable over a photographic lineup. In a live viewing or lineup, a victim, like me, could take into account a number of factors to aid in the identification—all calculated to prevent false identification. This was particularly crucial in my situation since I was familiar with the way *The* Weasel moved, the way he held his head, his voice and thus his mannerisms and idiosyncrasies. These would be dead giveaways as well as his general appearance. Tank's father told me that I was a brave girl, and after I was positioned on the window side of the two-way mirror, the lineup would proceed in the customary fashion.

Five men filed onto a stage-like platform in the room on the mirror side where I could see them but they couldn't see me. The wall behind the five men being observed had painted thereon a chart indicating measurements in feet and inches of the height of each participant. All of the participants were basically of the same height and bore a resemblance. Otherwise, the suspect would stand out like a wart on the end of the nose of a beauty queen and would be a dead give-away. At trial, my identification could be disregarded if it was deemed unduly suggestive.

Law enforcement, we later imagined, had a difficult time coming up with four other men as short as *The Weasel* and bearing similar features. They eventually put together a respectable group including a couple of police volunteers and two brothers, just barely five feet tall who had recently been arrested for shoplifting. The brothers' features matched that of *The Weasel* somewhat, so they were inserted in the line-up for that reason. They had shoulder length platinum blond hair, blue eyes and facial hair. Although they were quite a bit younger than *The Weasel,* they looked to be close to his age because their life styles had taken a heavy toll on their features. They did not walk. They swaggered in attempting to convey an air of superiority, no doubt due to their disdain for the criminal justice system. The brothers were nicknamed *Twiddle-Dee-Dumb* and *Twiddle-Dee-Dee* by detention personnel due to their lackadaisical attitude.

Another one of the participants included in the lineup, a probation officer by the name of Jimmy Davis, was shorter than *The Weasel* but other than that bore a striking resemblance. Another participant, Corbin Lucas, a man recruited off the street, was just plain scruffy by nature. His resemblance was also uncanny.

Tank's father told Tank later he was concerned about the lineup because *The* Weasel was not an easy match and he was afraid my identification might be deemed tainted by the across-the-board dissimilarities. *The Weasel,* one would have to admit, was pretty much a one of a kind. "*The Weasel's* mold must have been discarded the day he was created," Tank's father would later tell Tank. The rag-tag array of weasel lookalikes was paraded in front of the two-way mirror. Under other circumstances it would have been comical.

Even though the lookalikes could not see those of us who congregated behind the two-way mirror, they obviously knew they were the subject of scrutiny and played to their audience. *The Weasel* began exhibiting a nervous twitch as he stood facing the two-way mirror and then had one of his patented sneezing fits much like the one he apparently had in the middle of the heist at the bank. He also made a menacing gesture with his eyes, no doubt, surmising I was watching and might be dissuaded thereby in not making a positive identification.

I watched intently as the five men were paraded in front of me. I immediately recognized the man who had abducted me and held me captive. I couldn't help but smile as I looked into *The Weasel's* eyes knowing that his looks "could no longer kill" and that his bluff was as ineffective as the threatened bite of a gnat. Tank's father ordered the group to turn to the left, pause and then turn to the right. He asked each of them to step forward and recite the alphabet so that I could hear them speak. This was a mere formality, I was later told, as I, in my mind, had already identified my abductor. And this despite his physical transformation in an attempt to become unrecognizable.

When asked if I could identify anyone, I nodded and pointed at participant number 3, Willard Carsten, alias *The Weasel*, alias Wilber Smith, alias Santa. "That's the man who kidnapped me and held me hostage," I said without any hesitation. When asked if I was positive, I said "Yes, I would never forget those eyes or that face. They are forever etched in my mind. That is 'the man'!"

I was remarkably calm considering the circumstances. It was a fitting climax to an ordeal that no one should ever have to endure. The rest of the journey from this point forward, I anticipated, would be easier and I was confident I would have no difficulty in identifying my abductor in open court should I be required to do so.

I could hear my father and mother, who were seated on each side of me, breathe a sigh of relief. Although my father knew his reputation would be at stake, stated he was relieved that the kidnapper had been apprehended. Tank's father spoke into the intercom instructing that No. 3 be detained and the other participants be released or placed back into their jail cells. As everyone was preparing to leave, my father asked Tank's father if he could speak to him alone. Tank's father then took my father into an interview room and shut the door. We later learned that my father confessed to his involvement in the DNA testing and of having falsified the results. He said Tank's father did not appear to be shocked or judgmental and said he could see himself doing the same thing if faced with similar circumstances.

Tank's father then instructed my father to take our family home as he would be contacting the district attorney's office and providing them with a copy of my father's statement. My father said Tank's father then patted him on the shoulder, apparently in a sympathetic gesture, as the two parted and told him he would do everything in his power to dissuade the district attorney from filing criminal charges. He told my father, however, that the decision was not his and not a matter within his control. My father, in relating the incident later to my mother and me, said he understood and thanked Tank's father for his role in obtaining my release and the apprehension of *The Weasel*.

The Weasel was booked on kidnapping charges, an offense, which I later learned, could carry up to a life sentence in the penitentiary. True to form, *The Weasel*, it was said, threw his weaselly fit, thrashing about claiming a frame-up, the prosecution of an innocent person and a case of mistaken identification. He was placed in a holding cell to await his arraignment not only on the kidnap charge, but also the following charges: false imprisonment, assault, burglary, robbery, theft, fraud, extortion, eluding, and of course, false impersonation. Tank told me that they "threw the book" at him.

We were told *The Weasel* would also be facing federal charges in connection with the bank robbery and the interstate transportation of a kidnap victim across state lines, and because the bank money had been confiscated and placed in evidence, he was unable to hire a lawyer or even post bond. His evil ways had netted him nothing but heartache and distress. *The Weasel* now had nothing but time on his hands. Unfortunately, that was not something he could use to post bond or take to the bank. He had reached the end of the line, so to speak, and would now have to wallow in the mire of his ways.

After my father left, Tank's father, we were told, went to the district attorney's office and met with Mitchell Kino, the prosecuting attorney who had filed the criminal charges against *The Weasel* and was otherwise familiar with the case. Tank's father then provided the prosecutor with a copy of my father's confession wherein my father had admitted to having falsified the DNA results on the items collected from the bank robbery. He explained that my father was being blackmailed by *The Weasel* and that my father believed my life was in jeopardy, and therefore, being under duress, falsified the results.

It is told, Kino thereupon presented a solution to Tank's father. He suggested they charge my father with two offenses: Tampering with Evidence and Falsifying Records and give my father a two-year deferred judgment and sentence. This meant that if my father pleaded guilty to the charges and complied with all the terms and conditions of the deferred judgment and sentence, at the end of the two-year period his plea could then be withdrawn and the case dismissed. That way, it was explained, my father would have no criminal record. On the other hand, if he did *not* comply, which, of course, was very unlikely, then a conviction would enter and my father would then be sentenced. Tank's father felt that was a fair disposition. And since, it was tantamount to a dismissal, my father readily entered into the plea agreement. "The only difference between a complete dismissal now or one later was two years," my father would later explain. There are times when the end justifies the means. Sometimes you have to take a detour to reach your destination!"

When *The Weasel* was arraigned on the criminal charge of false impersonation, he sneered and looked at Judge Sheriden with contempt. To impersonate Santa Claus was the least serious but the most problematic of all the charges. Although being Santa's alter ego was an exception under certain circumstances and not considered a crime, what *The Weasel* did in the instant case was considered a despicable act and one that was inexcusable. To impersonate Santa Claus for a worthy cause was one thing, but to impersonate Santa Claus for evil purposes was an unforgivable sin.

The Weasel, no doubt, could see the writing on the wall. In exchange for pleading guilty to the major charges, the charge of false impersonation surprisingly was dropped and *The Weasel* received a combined sentence of ninety-six years. Because of his age, *The Weasel* would be spending the rest of his natural life behind bars wishing he had made better choices. He later would tell the prison chaplain he, at last, realized there were no short-cuts in life and that to circumvent the law was a recipe for disaster. In the end, to *The Weasel's* credit, he blamed only himself.

CHAPTER SEVEN
GREATEST GIFT OF ALL

Throughout the ages there has been a controversy brewing over the existence of Santa Claus. Because no one has seen the jolly old man but only replicas, there are the doubters—those who because they have not seen do not believe. Yet, there are those who have been beneficiaries of Santa's wondrous deeds and find that to be proof enough of Santa's existence. They argue that just because you can't see or feel air, doesn't mean air doesn't exist.

The *R*U*1*2s*, for the most part, were believers. However, their vision was distorted somewhat by *The Weasel's* false impersonation of a good and kindly man whose image in Jefferson City had been severely tarnished. It was against this backdrop that I arose early Christmas morning the year of my abduction to see for myself whether Santa was real or a figment of my imagination as some of my friends had suggested.

I was a realist. However, there was always that lingering doubt. So, when I counted six chimes from the old grandfather's clock in the downstairs hallway, I could wait no longer. Tip toeing my way past the open door of my parents' bedroom and down the carpeted staircase that led into the hallway leading to the den, I caught the glimpse of something shiny. It was the reflection of the Christmas tree lights on the chrome handlebars of a ruby-red girl's bicycle sparkling like a gem in the otherwise dim-lit room.

I had a bicycle—a hand-me-down from my cross-town cousin. The same was true of a tricycle I had when I was a little girl and before that a kiddie cart. In fact, many of my toys came from Camille who was then a high school senior. I was envious of those who always received new. I could scarcely believe my eyes as I stared at the shiny new spoked two-wheeler in front of me.

"Looks like Santa has been here," I heard my father say behind me. Now standing in the doorway of the den were both my father and mother. "Merry Christmas, Darling," I heard my mother say. "We didn't mean to startle you."

I remember just staring at the sparkling ruby-red bicycle that dominated the den unable to find the right words to reflect my amazement. Finally, I managed to say, "You shouldn't have."

My mother and father had stunned looks on their faces and stared at each other with what might be described as quizzical expressions. Neither said anything as they ventured into the room and hastened to inspect the ruby-red bicycle. As they opened one of the saddle bags hanging from the rear fender rack, they retrieved an envelope.

"Look," my father said to me. "There is an envelope with your name written on it."

"What do you suppose....?" My mother asked, not really finishing her question. Looking at me, my mother handed me the envelope. The seal on the back of the envelope bore the initials "SC."

I broke the seal and retrieved a letter that had been folded in half. Carefully unfolding it, I read to myself the contents thereof.

Dear Shacoo,

It was with regret that I learned of the deplorable acts of someone purporting to represent me. I assure you the imposter had no authority. You were a most brave young lady to have endured the tribulations with which you were forced to face. You are truly an inspiration to us all. This shiny new ruby-red bicycle is yours. It was made at my workshop. It is one of a kind as are you. 'Shacoo,' as among the angels in heaven, means 'I love you.' You, therefore, are preordained or destined to share the profound love within you for the betterment of humankind. Never forget the true meaning of Christmas and its promise of everlasting peace and joy. May your journey in life be everything you expect and deserve.

Love,
Santa

My parents, concerned about the origination of the ruby-red bicycle, inspected the snow surrounding our home only to find that it was undisturbed. "There are no tracks indicating a method of delivery," I still remember my father saying. Grabbing each other's hand with a grip conveying disbelief, my parents admitted later they searched for an answer that had eluded them all their lives. "Could there be?" they both said they pondered as they stared into the endless expanse of sky and followed the flight patterns of the occasional snow crystals as they fell aimlessly from the heavens to a somber earth below—no two crystals the same. If only they had asked me, I could have told them. My answer? *Of course, there is a Santa. Life itself is a gift. It is a benefit we receive every second of every minute of every hour of every day. It is a gift that keeps on giving! One that cannot be readily explained. But, one that is there nonetheless.*

BEING DISCOVERED WAS NOT AN OPTION...

BLUE

THE NEW R·U·1·2 ADVENTURE

BY JUDITH BLEVINS AND
CARROLL MULTZ

COMING FEBRUARY 2017

THE
CHILDHOOD LEGENDS™
SERIES

ABOUT THE AUTHORS

udith Blevins' whole professional life has been centered in and around the courts and the criminal justice system. Her experience in having been a court clerk and having served under five consecutive district attorneys in Grand Junction, Colorado, has provided the fodder for her novels. She has had a daily dose of mystery, intrigue and courtroom drama over the years and her novels share all with her readers.

arroll Multz, a trial lawyer for over forty years, a former two-term district attorney, assistant attorney general, and judge, has been involved in cases ranging from municipal courts to and including the United States Supreme Court. His high profile cases have been reported in the *New York Times, Redbook Magazine* and various police magazines. He was one of the attorneys in the *Columbine Copycat Case* that occurred in Fort Collins, Colorado, in 2001 that was featured by Barbara Walters on *ABC's 20/20*. Now retired, he is an Adjunct Professor at Colorado Mesa University in Grand Junction, Colorado, teaching law-related courses at both the graduate and undergraduate levels.

THE CHILDHOOD LEGENDS™ SERIES
THE FIRST R*U*1*2 ADVENTURE
OPERATION
CAT TALE
BY JUDITH BLEVINS AND
CARROLL MULTZ
AVAILABLE IN PAPERBACK & EBOOK

www.ingramcontent.com/pod-product-compliance
Lightning Source LLC
Chambersburg PA
CBHW030538130626
46552CB00006B/2317